MAN OF THE SHADOWS

By Don Coldsmith

Fiction

MAN OF THE SHADOWS

FOLLOW THE WIND

THE ELK-DOG HERITAGE

BUFFALO MEDICINE

TRAIL OF THE SPANISH BIT

Nonfiction

HORSIN' AROUND AGAIN

HORSIN' AROUND

MAN OF THE SHADOWS

DON COLDSMITH

DOUBLEDAY & COMPANY, INC.

GARDEN CITY, NEW YORK

1983

Library of Congress Cataloging in Publication Data

Coldsmith, Don, 1926–
Man of the shadows.

I. Title.
PS3553.O445M3   1983   813'.54
ISBN: 0-385-18091-8
Library of Congress Catalog Card Number 82–46078

First Edition

MAN OF THE SHADOWS

INTRODUCTION

When darkness has fallen on the prairie and the story fires are lighted, young and old gather to exchange tales of "how it came to be." Each tribe has its favorite versions of why the eagle is bald, how the bobcat lost his tail, why prairie dogs are brown.

And, among all tribes, there is a legendary supernatural figure, the Trickster. He is called by many names. For the Kiowa he is Uncle Saindi, for the Crows Old Man Coyote. The Sioux call him Grandfather Iktoemi, the Blackfeet Old Man Napi, and the Cheyenne Old Man Wihio. His character is always the same. Whimsical and prankish, he can hurt you or help you.

In Kiowa legend, he is the semideity who opened a hole to the underworld through which buffalo came to populate the plains. On the other hand, when the rawhide lashing on the lodge pole slips and the nearly erected lodge collapses, that is the work of the mischievous Trickster.

Descriptions are much the same from tribe to tribe. He is tall, ungainly, almost ugly, with a big nose, long hair, and piercing black eyes. His garments are varied but always outlandish. He is very old, maybe older than the earth. Even the Trickster himself has forgotten.

He can change himself at will into an animal, a tree, a fish, or any other being, even a rock, or he may choose to become invisible.

He speaks all languages, those of men and those of the animals. For hours at a time, he can exchange news and gossip with a babbling stream. When the wind sighs in the tops of the cottonwoods, it is speaking to him:

"Good day to you, Uncle!"

And he answers back in the same tongue.

You may sit on the top of a grassy hill on a still day and watch little stray puffs of breeze move the heavy seed heads of prairie grasses in the Moon of Ripening. You may have the intuitive feeling that it marks the course of some unseen living thing, and you may be correct. The movement may well be the stirring of the grasses caused by the passing of the Trickster.

Or you may trace the erratic dance of a wisp of dust across a still dry flat. Some call these dust devils, but the people of the prairie know that it is the Trickster at play.

Did you ever feel that someone was watching from behind you? You turn quickly, and from the corner of your eye you *almost* catch a glimpse of a fleeting shadow among the sumac on the hillside. Then there is nothing there. The Trickster was watching.

He is a constant traveler, swift as the wings of the prairie wind, and he may be anywhere, ready for a mischievous prank or a helping hand.

One custom is universal among all the tribes with legends of the Trickster. His stories must always be told at night, preferably by the flickering light of the fire, because long ago, he commanded it so.

To the People, he is the Old Man of the Shadows.

CHAPTER 1

There was nothing that morning, as the People started on the hunt, to indicate that it would be different from any other.

Eagle, young warrior of the Elk-dog band, was uncommonly satisfied with the world and with his part in it. The Moon of Ripening was his favorite time of the year. Prairie flowers of brilliant yellow and purple dotted the rolling hills in profusion. Eagle loved the smell of the season, with warm days and crisp cool nights. These nights were so delicious in which to curl closely to a warm and affectionate wife.

He smiled to himself at the thought of Sweet Grass, mother of his son, Bobcat, and his daughter, Little Eagle. Just now, she waited in the valley behind the hunters. She, with the others of the butchering party, would wait until the hunters returned with news of the kill. Then would begin the days of processing the meat and skins of the buffalo, preparing for the coming winter.

It had always been so among the People. Back beyond the memory of the grandparents of the oldest of the tribe, the People had been buffalo hunters. Of course, in this generation, the hunt was easier. Shortly before Eagle's birth, the People had acquired the horse—elk-dogs—on which the hunter might ride to pursue the shifting herds. He was proud of the fact that his own, the Southern band, had been the first to initiate the use of the animals. In fact, they were now referred to as the Elk-dog band by the rest of the tribe, because of their expertise with the horse.

Eagle was doubly proud that the first horse the People had

seen had been that ridden by his own father, Heads Off. An outsider, a member of a far-off tribe with hairy faces, the young warrior had married into the tribe and was now undeniably one of the People. His powerful elk-dog medicine was embodied in a shiny device that could be placed in a horse's mouth to control it.

Heads Off had taught this medicine to the young men, and the results had been far-reaching. Where previously the hunters had been forced to pursue the buffalo on foot, they now learned the use of the bow and the lance on horseback. The People had acquired more horses and had emerged as a strong and affluent group on the plains.

Even their hated and feared enemy, the Head Splitters, now treated the People with caution and respect. Since the elk-dog medicine, there was no question that life had been easier. With more food, the children were fat and the women happy. There were jokes that a new name was needed for the Moon of Hunger, for now supplies remained adequate through the winter. Heads Off had become a band chief after the death in battle of old Hump Ribs. Eagle had heard the story many times.

Yes, he was proud of his heritage. His link with foreign blood was shown by the fringe of fur on his upper lip and along his jaw. He was proud, but not arrogant about it. Eagle had always been well-liked, had been popular even as a child. He could call nearly everyone in the tribe by name and had many friends.

His brother Owl had had more difficulty in adjusting to their difference from other children. Owl had apprenticed himself to the medicine man. The more private, withdrawn life of the mystic seer was more suited to Owl's quiet personality. He was rapidly becoming a highly respected practitioner of his art.

Eagle's thoughts returned abruptly to the matter at hand. Standing Bird, ahead of him, was motioning the others forward but cautioning quiet. They moved carefully toward the crest of the ridge, spreading as they did so. The horses picked their way up the slope, through the rubble of limestone outcropping. Seed heads of the tall real-grass, now turning reddish in its ripening stages, waved and brushed gently against Eagle's elbows. Heavy yellow heads of feathery plume grass, almost as tall, nodded aside as they passed.

It was a good year for the growth of the grasses, and buffalo had been present in large numbers. Now scouts had reported a massive herd, quietly grazing in the area. Plans had been made for a great hunt, one last drive before the onslaught of Cold Maker. Nearly all the men of the band would be involved, except those too aged or infirm, and a contingent of the Bowstring Society. These would remain available to defend the camp.

Eagle glanced to each side as the scattered line of horsemen neared the crest. Standing Bird had dropped back to a position on Eagle's left. Beyond him rode Red Dog, a flamboyant young subchief, leader of the Blood Society. To the right, not far down the line, rode Heads Off himself.

Bothered by the aching-bones affliction as the years progressed, Eagle's father rarely joined in routine hunts. But this was a special occasion, a beautiful day, and Eagle knew that the chief simply could not sit in camp. He still sat his horse well and carried the lance most convincingly.

Still beyond, Eagle could see the spotted horse of his uncle. Long Elk was one of the Elk-dog Society, the warrior society to which Eagle himself belonged.

There was a thrill, a racing in his blood, as he looked up and down the line. Eagle was proud of his tribe, capable, dependable warriors and hunters, his friends and teachers. He was proud to be a man of the People, glorying in the strength of his young manhood. This would be a great hunt.

Had not Owl, the medicine man, said so? After his dance and vision, he had cast the bones and predicted a great kill.

The tiny skittering objects, tossed on the painted skin, could tell much to one trained in such things. And there was no question. Owl was good at his profession. He had been well trained by White Buffalo, the most capable of medicine men. In addition, Owl had traveled far and seen other medicines at work. His body still bore marks of captivity by strange far-away tribes.

So Eagle knew it was to be a good day. Owl had said so, and Owl's buffalo medicine was known to be perfectly accurate.

Only a slight doubt assailed him as the riders neared the crest of the hill. There was Owl's warning.

The young medicine man had approached his brother just as Eagle swung to the back of his gray stallion.

"Eagle, you must be careful."

"I am always careful, my brother!"

He hefted his lance and settled himself comfortably on his saddle pad.

"I know. But today be especially so."

Owl was so serious that Eagle stopped and took a long look into his eyes. As always, there was that faraway, unfathomable depth in the medicine man's gaze. It was as if he looked through and beyond, seeing things not meant for ordinary men. Eagle was uncomfortable, as he always was under his brother's scrutiny. He spoke insistently, almost sharply.

"Owl, is there something I should know?"

"I do not know, my brother. The signs are good, but there is a shadow. I do not understand all I see."

He shrugged and smiled sheepishly, a little embarrassed.

"Perhaps it is nothing. Only, be very careful, my brother."

"Of course!"

Eagle nodded cheerfully and kneed his horse forward to where the hunting party was forming at the edge of the meadow.

CHAPTER 2

The long line of hunters crested the ridge almost together. A rolling plain unfolded before them, the ripening grasses of the prairie dotted with innumerable buffalo. The shaggy animals grazed calmly, not yet excited, as the horsemen drew nearer at a walk. It was understood that no one would move faster until their quarry started to run.

"*Aiee*, there are many!" Eagle spoke softly to Standing Bird on his left.

The other nodded.

"It should be a great hunt."

The hunters would kill all they were able. Any excess beyond the needs of the band could be converted into robes and pemmican for trade with the Growers. These river-dwelling people raised substantial quantities of corn and pumpkins, trading with the hunting tribes for meat and skins.

A wary old cow raised her head to sniff the air nervously. She sensed that all was not quite right and lowed softly to her calf. Still, the animal seemed not to connect her premonition of danger with the mounted figures approaching. She was relying on her sense of smell, more acute than her vision. The hunters, knowing this characteristic, had approached upwind, and the animals had not yet caught the scent.

The cow nervously paced a few steps, then started uncertainly toward the rest of the herd. A yearling bull threw up his head, caught a stray scent on a shifting puff of breeze, and trotted toward the others.

The hunters were now within striking distance. Long Elk,

leader of the hunt, raised his lance to signal the charge, and the hunters moved smoothly to a trot, then a canter, and finally a full gallop. The buffalo started to run, their lumbering gait deceptively fast.

Eagle urged his horse forward. It was one of the best, a gray stallion from the mare Lolita, the original elk-dog brought by his father when he came to the People. The gray responded to the slightest pressure of the knees, and moved into the charge effortlessly and smoothly. Eagle felt the thrill, as he always did, of a fine horse under him. It was a good day, a good life.

He singled out a fat two-year-old cow for his quarry. The horse identified the chosen animal almost instantly, and pressed forward. They approached the running animal from the left rear, allowing efficient use of the lance. The razor-sharp flint point entered the exposed flank, ranging forward and down, into the chest cavity.

When the horse felt the shock of impact, he came to a sliding stop. The momentum of the stumbling cow allowed retrieval of Eagle's lance, and he kneed the horse forward again, past the dying cow. He cast hardly a glance at the animal, locked in the death struggle, with bloody froth from punctured lungs spewing from the flared nostrils. Eagle was looking for his next target.

A young bull galloped wildly by, and the horse lunged forward again. The kill was not quite so cleanly accomplished, but it was adequate, and the bull fell, to lie kicking in the dust. Eagle glanced quickly around to see how others were doing.

Here and there lay a fallen carcass, and the hunters were methodically striking more. Most of the men carried lances, but some preferred the bow. An arrow from the short stout plains bow of the People could send an arrow completely through a running buffalo.

Eagle turned and made another rush at a passing cow. He

had secured four animals altogether before his movements brought him to a slight rise, where he could see better the entire shape of the hunt.

A highly desirable thing had happened. The hunters had encountered the herd in a bowl-shaped meadow, out of sight and smell of the main herd. Perhaps a hundred animals, instead of running directly toward the other thousands beyond the hill, were circling. The meadow was the extent of their world for the moment, and they milled around and around, not yet completely excited, more puzzled at the strange happenings.

Aiee, it was as Owl had said! It would be a great hunt. Other hunters had seen the circumstance and were taking advantage of it. Riders circled outside the perimeter of the milling herd, attempting to turn animals back if they broke away. Only if an animal succeeded in escape was it pursued.

The excitement was calming down. It would be well to move slowly, act deliberately, so as not to panic the herd. There would now be more time to be deliberate.

An idea occurred to Eagle. He had been training a new buffalo horse, and this would be an ideal time to complete the animal's education. He had left the mare back beyond the ridge with the rest of the party, in the care of Sweet Grass.

"Standing Bird!" he called softly. "I go to get my other horse!"

The other man nodded and waved, understanding the reasoning involved.

Quickly Eagle urged the gray over the ridge, pounded along the back trail to where the others waited, the obvious question in their eyes.

"*Aiee*, it is a great kill," he announced enthusiastically. "The herd is circling. We may be all day at the hunt."

There was a scattered grumble from those impatient to begin the butchering, but most were delighted.

Already, Eagle was stripping the saddle from the gray.

Sweet Grass led the spotted mare forward, and he hastily saddled and swung up, after a quick embrace. He urged the animal forward, cresting the ridge at a fast canter, and then
reined in so as not to alarm the herd.

The mare was skittish for a little, prancing nervously at the
dust, motion, and the heavy animal smell of the buffalo. She
soon settled, and Eagle took his place in the circle next to
Standing Bird. The older man nodded approval.

"She will do well, Eagle!"

A yearling bull broke from the milling herd and started toward the ridge, tail up and at a gallop. Eagle reined his horse
around to follow.

The spotted mare was a bit slow in pursuit, due to inexpe-
rience. Again, after the lance struck true, Eagle was a trifle
slow in retrieving, since the mare was not adept at her sliding
stop. The shaft was almost twisted from his grip, but after a
moment he recovered and started at a trot back toward the
milling circle.

He was only a few paces from the outer perimeter when
there was a sudden lunge by an old cow. Her half-grown calf
and a young bull joined her, and the three bolted almost
directly toward the young man. Standing Bird shouted a warning. The spotted mare, feeling no great threat until now, suddenly panicked. She wheeled to escape from the approach of
the strange-smelling shaggy beasts. Eagle was unable to control her frightened retreat and could only do his best to remain
on the back of the lunging animal.

Straight for the top of the ridge the runaway sprinted, unable to escape the pursuing terror. Eagle thought for a moment of jumping off to take his chances with the running animals behind. He glanced back and saw with alarm that the
herd had ceased to circle and was breaking away, beginning to
bolt past the hunters to follow the first three animals. If he
jumped now, he would likely be trampled by the rush. He had

lost his chance, and it was now too late. He must stay with the mare at all costs and ride until she calmed enough for him to regain control.

They topped the ridge, the increasing thunder close behind. Spread before him, Eagle saw the innumerable buffalo of the main herd, scattered as far as the eye could see. He braced himself, expecting the mare to turn aside from this new threat. To his surprise, the fear-crazed horse bolted straight ahead, nearly colliding with a grazing bull. The animal threw up his head in astonishment, unchewed grass hanging from a corner of his mouth. Then he began to run.

In the space of a few heartbeats, other animals jumped and ran, as the scent of panic drifted through the herd. The earth began to vibrate with the thunder of thousands of hooves. The sound increased, until it seemed the whole earth was shaking. In a moment, Eagle and his frightened mare were completely surrounded by running animals. There could be no turning aside now, not even if he could regain control of the horse. There was nowhere to go. As far as he could see in any direction there was only a sea of heaving backs.

Eagle recalled for a moment that Two Dogs, the false medicine man, had been killed in such a stampede. The People had been unable even to find his body. It had been completely destroyed and scattered by the myriad of sharp black hooves. If the mare stumbled, it would be the same with the body of Eagle.

For the present, he must give the mare her head, let her run with the herd, hopefully to slow when the buffalo did. And that, Eagle was afraid, might be a very long time. He glanced at Sun Boy's torch, barely past the highest point in his daily run. How long would Eagle's strength allow him to hold on?

The mare's gallop slowed to a steady beating rhythm, better than the panicky pounding at the beginning. She was pacing herself to the speed of the buffalo. The animals still crowded closely against them, pressing against Eagle's legs and the flanks of the mare, but she seemed less frightened now. If only she didn't stumble.

A forgotten thought flitted through Eagle's mind. This must be the danger Owl had warned of. He would tell his brother about it when he got back.

CHAPTER 3

It seemed like days that the herd had been running. Eagle knew it could not be, because Sun Boy was still high, but he was exhausted. His arms and legs ached, and his body was numb from the pounding. He knew the mare was tiring, too. She had stumbled and nearly fallen a little while ago.

His mind was becoming confused, and he imagined at times that he was already dead. He had crossed into a world composed entirely of stampeding buffalo, in which he must ride forever. Then the painful cramps in his legs would bring him back to unpleasant reality.

After a time Eagle realized that he could tell something of what lay ahead by the change in sound. An upcoming field of broken rock scattered among the grasses produced a clattering sound from the animals ahead, moments before his mare arrived. He would tense himself for an expected fall, but so far the animal had maintained her footing.

When he first noticed a new change in the rumble ahead, he was unable to identify it for some time. The earthshaking thunder still continued, but there was now less thunder directly ahead. Almost at the same time he noticed animals ahead veering to the left, as if startled. Some attempted to stop, bracing their feet in vain as the oncoming ranks pushed them forward or trampled them into the ground.

The mare stumbled over the body of a buffalo, nearly fell, and scrambled over the obstacle. Then Eagle could see ahead and realized the danger in the situation. The stampeding herd had come to the bluff overlooking the river. Some unfortunate individuals were being pushed over the edge by those behind.

In the old days, before the horse, the People had sometimes deliberately tried to stampede the herds over a bluff. The resulting pileup of dead and injured buffalo would produce needed meat and robes.

Desperately Eagle tried to pull the mare to the left with those animals that were making the turn. He had nearly managed the change in direction when a gigantic bull pushed through the film of dust, unseeing, uncaring. It crashed against other animals in its way, blundering straight ahead, unaware of the danger.

Eagle struck out at the buffalo, kicked its face, yelled and screamed, but the animal would not turn. The great bull lowered his massive head and pushed forward, pushing the mare and her rider sideways toward the brink. The mare fought for her footing for a moment, then stepped off into emptiness. Illogically, Eagle clung tightly to her mane as they fell.

He was aware of the first impact, dimly aware that he had struck the body of one of the earlier victims of the fall. He had a sensation of bouncing and barely time to wonder desperately how he could possibly escape being crushed by the fall of ensuing bodies over the bluff. Then something struck him behind the left ear, and the world exploded into darkness.

When Eagle returned to consciousness, darkness was still his first sensation. It was immediately followed, however, by an overwhelming sensation of pain. His entire body consisted of one dull ache, augmented by sharp, stabbing pains in various portions of his battered anatomy. His left leg, right ribs, and his head throbbed with a knifelike thrust at each heartbeat.

He tried to look around in the dimness. There were the bulky shapes of buffalo carcasses, partly in and partly out of the water. There was feeble movement from a mortally injured animal at the base of the bluff, but for the most part all was quiet.

Painfully, Eagle turned his head, attempting to orient himself. In what must be the west, a reddish glow still hung in the sky. Sun Boy had reached the earth's rim, painted himself red, and extinguished his torch to go to his lodge on the other side for the night.

At the opposite horizon, the full red Moon of Ripening was sliding into view. Its light would help him to see more of his predicament, Eagle hoped. He resolved to watch it until its entire circle was visible, but it was no use. He drifted off again, dimly aware that there were rocks and gravel under him, uncomfortably gouging into his injured back.

The next time he awoke, the full moon was directly overhead, and the entire landscape was bathed in silvery light. Momentarily, Eagle wondered, as he had all his life, how the fullness of the fat red moon could change so rapidly to small and silvery white. It was of little consequence now.

The young man looked around, attempting to evaluate the situation. He was lying on his back on a narrow gravel bar, partially in the water. He must have been thrown clear in the fall, away from the carcasses of dying animals which he saw piled against the base of the cliff. He felt the chill of the night, but the water itself was warm to his right leg. He looked at his painfully throbbing left leg and saw with sudden alarm that it was not shaped properly. His sense of position told him that the leg was extended straight out before him. Yet, his eyes revealed that impression to be incorrect. The moccasined foot jutted crazily at right angles to the leg, from a point halfway below his knee.

Anxiously, Eagle sat up, oblivious to the tearing pains in the rest of his body, in his anxiety over the broken leg. Carefully he felt the bone through the buckskin of his legging. There was a hard projecting lump where none should be. That would be the broken bone. But had it burst through the skin? It was essential to know.

He fumbled at his waist for his flint knife, fortunately still in its sheath. He slit the buckskin and saw with great relief that there was no white bone to gleam in the moonlight. The skin was intact. He sank back in relief. It was well known to the People that bad spirits could enter through such a hole in the skin over a bone. The injured person would become weaker and finally die as the spirits devoured him from within. At least, Eagle did not have that worry. Exhausted from the exertion, he drifted into a troubled half sleep again.

At his next awakening, Eagle was able to think more clearly. He attempted to reconstruct the previous events. The moon was still high, and the night's chill had become deeper.

He knew that the buffalo had carried him half a day's journey from the People. They would look for him, of course, but would likely be unsuccessful. There would be no way to track, and even the direction of travel would be in question, obliterated by a thousand trampling hooves. He could count on no help from his people.

His immediate concern was the leg. It must be straightened. Very carefully, to be sure. A chance move could still poke the sharp spicules of bone through the skin. Gingerly, painfully, he sat up again. Mustering courage, he took the errant foot with both hands and swung it quickly into position. The foot seemed wooden for a moment, but then the stab of pain struck like a bolt of real-fire in a storm, flashing up the leg, through his body, and smashing against the base of his skull.

For a moment, Eagle thought he would faint, then wished that he could. The injured foot would not stay upright, but kept rotating, the toe pointing to the left. Almost frantic from the pain involved, Eagle snatched at fist-sized stones from the gravel bar around him, piling them around the foot to keep it in position, toe pointing upward. There was a sort of relief when he managed to immobilize it.

He sank back again, wishing for daylight. Somehow, he must manage to bind the leg in position. But with what? He still had no clear idea of how he could accomplish the task. Again he drifted into fitful, half-fainting slumber from the monumental exertion.

CHAPTER 4

When Eagle awoke again, it was dawn. Heavy banks of fog hung over the plain, and he had become chilled. The river itself seemed to smolder. Smoky vapors rose from its surface. Again he had the feeling of unreality, that he was in another world. Could that be true? Had he crossed over into the Spirit-World?

The raucous clatter of a trio of crows downstream reached his ears. Arguing over some disagreement of their own, the birds made him doubt that he had crossed over. If so, this must be much like the world he had so recently departed. He cautiously raised to an elbow, and the pain removed all doubt. One could not hurt if he were dead.

And above all, Eagle did hurt. His entire body was one massive pain. He thought of the broken leg and raised up to look at it, propped among the stones. Now that the shattered limb was in alignment, much of the pain had stopped. There was only a dull, wooden ache. Cautiously, he moved the other leg, then his arms. He found no other serious damage. His ears throbbed, and he realized that he must have received a blow to the head. He located a bump behind the left ear, crusted with dried blood. The area was tender but seemed intact. Apparently the leg was the major injury.

Eagle looked around, seeking to orient himself and further evaluate his predicament. His gravel bar, he now saw, jutted out from the bank opposite the river's bluff. His position, surrounded by water on three sides, was on the tip of a fingerlike projection of shifting gravel. It had been deposited there at last flood time and would be gone again with the next heavy rain. At least, it was good that it had been available. He might have drowned if the bar had not been there.

At this thought, he looked again across the strip of water. Dozens of buffalo carcasses lay piled at the base of the bluff, partly in and partly out of the river. A thought struck him, an unanswered question. How could he have been thrown so far? It seemed impossible. Had he managed, in a semiconscious state, to swim to safety? Surely, he would remember something of the ordeal.

Perhaps he had held to his horse's mane by instinct, and the mare had floundered across, to run away after losing her unconscious rider. He would have to think more about it later, but just now thinking seemed to increase the pain in his head.

He looked farther along the stream. He lay at the head of a shallow riffle, but upstream the river stretched on until lost in the fog, a still, deep water. It was bordered on his left by the bluff, and on his right by a scrubby strip of willows and cottonwoods. An occasional stately sycamore bent knobby knees to stick its sprawling feet into the dark stream.

Downstream, beyond the riffle, the scene repeated itself, until lost in a distant bend of the river.

Directly in front of him, on the shore side, the fog was dense in the little strip of woods. Eagle could begin to see the glowing ball of fire that was Sun Boy's torch, struggling in the east to burn away the fog. So far, it was only perceived as a yellowish blob in the blue white of the fog. Soon Sun Boy would overcome the chill and dampness, climbing high on his daily run. Until then, Eagle would be cold and uncomfortable.

Again, he looked upstream and saw that visibility was improving. Stray puffs of breeze were clearing the fog along the water's surface, and he saw that there was actually considerable current in the apparently still water.

Some scattered debris was being carried along, and he recognized a few sticks from the night's work of a beaver. In a moment, he became quite interested in the floating sticks. Here perhaps would be the needed materials to splint his broken leg. Fascinated, he watched the leafy trash drift with agonizing slowness toward his gravel bar. He stretched as far as he could, reaching, trying to grasp the sticks before they were sucked into the swift water of the riffle to be swept away.

He frantically seized a long stick and used it to drag smaller ones to shore. In a short while, Eagle had accumulated a handful of green cottonwood cuttings as thick as his thumb and varying in length from a hand's span to as long as his arm. He discarded those crooked or leafy ones, but still was exuberant over his success. Strange, he thought, how a handful of sticks could become the most important thing in one's life. Now what to bind them with?

He looked longingly at the wealth of materials across the river, the hides of many buffalo. They would be ideal for the purpose, but might as well be on the other side of the earth. He could not reach them with his broken leg flopping loosely. The very thought of the grinding ends of shattered bone made him wince.

Then, as if in answer to his need, he saw upstream another floating object. At first he could not identify it, but then made out the rounded outline of an animal's body. It was a buffalo calf, drowned or killed in the fall from the bluff.

Slowly, so slowly, the floating body moved, sometimes seeming hardly to progress at all. Eagle was ready with his stick long before it was needed. He had decided that he must have the drifting calf, at whatever the cost. Its skin could help bind his leg, and the flesh would furnish food. He was prepared to throw himself into the water if necessary, in spite of the pain to his injured leg.

As it happened, it was not necessary. The drifting carcass circled gently and, as if guided precisely, came to rest against the bank, well within reach of his grasping hands.

In a matter of moments, his knife was stripping skin from

the dead calf. Working mostly by logic, Eagle padded the injured leg with a square of hide, the soft fur toward his own skin. Then the beaver sticks were applied and lashed tightly in place with strips of calfskin. He wondered for a moment if the binding would be too tight when the rawhide dried. Ah, well, never mind. He could always loosen it or cut it and retie.

Satisfied, Eagle now attempted to rise. If he could reach the trees and cut a sturdier stick to lean on, he would be able to move about more easily. He looked up toward his goal. The fog was breaking up now, and it was possible to see more readily into and among the sparse strip of timber.

He stopped in amazement. There, only a few steps away, burned a tiny campfire. Eagle was certain it had not been there earlier. Still, the slight breeze had been from the other direction. In the fog and in his preoccupation with his pain, he might not have noticed, until the fog lifted.

A man was squatting near the fire, cooking meat on sticks over the coals. The stranger glanced up, seemed not at all surprised to see the crippled Eagle.

"Come," he beckoned, using the universal hand-sign language, "the meat is almost ready."

Instinctively, Eagle's hand touched the knife at his waist. How could he have been so completely unaware of the stranger's presence? He was angry with himself, irritated that he had been so vulnerable without even knowing. His resentment was now directed at this man, a stranger who had witnessed his shameful incompetence. In addition, the other man might be a real threat. He had not yet seen any indication of the man's identity.

Eagle stood, swaying unsteadily, balanced on one leg and the beaver stick, hand still on his knife. The stranger, puttering around the fire, glanced up at him again.

"Put your knife away. Come and sit!" The man spoke aloud, and the tone of his voice was a trifle impatient. Somehow, Eagle felt like a chastened child, and he hobbled forward to obey the command of the other. Droplets of sweat beaded his face, as the pain of exertion swept over him with every lurching movement. He was determined not to reveal the extent of his weakness to the stranger.

It was not until he had settled himself against the trunk of a giant sycamore that his mind began to function again, after a fashion. His teeth were still tightly clenched against the weakness and the knifelike pain in his injured leg. He took a few deep breaths and began to observe the other man with curiosity and still with some resentment. The stranger had irritated him by the patronizing tone of the command. By what right, Eagle fumed inwardly to himself, does he order me to do anything? Yet it had seemed natural to obey, and Eagle had done so without question.

Then a curious thought struck him. The first communication from the stranger had been in the sign language. Any of the tribes of the prairie, or even beyond, could have communicated in this way. But the second, the terse impatient command from the other, had been a spoken phrase. Since Eagle had understood it, it must have been spoken in his own tongue, that of the People. Puzzled, he thought the matter over again. Yes, the short speech had been completely without accent, so smoothly spoken that Eagle had accepted it without even a question.

Now questions came leaping. Who was this stranger, camping alone on the prairie, who spoke the language of the People flawlessly? He was certainly not of the Elk-dog band. Could he be of the Northern band, or possibly the Mountain band?

Eastern band, more likely, Eagle told himself with an inward smile. The Eastern band had always carried a reputation for foolish ways. There were many jokes among the other bands, about the ineptness of that group. Certainly, camping alone in the vastness of the prairie showed no great powers of judgment. But all this was merely whimsy.

"Uncle," asked Eagle politely, "you speak my tongue. Are you of the People?"

The piercing black eyes gazed at the younger man for a long moment. Eagle was reminded somehow of the gaze of his brother Owl, the medicine man. Finally, the other spoke:

"No. I have no tribe."

Aiee! An outcast, a man rejected by his tribe. Expelled, perhaps, for some infraction of the rules of some tribal council long ago. Sometimes such a man joined another tribe, sometimes attempted to live as a solitary recluse. That, apparently, in this case.

But survival of a lone outcast would be unusual. Eagle wished to know more. His questions were interrupted by the stranger, who now lifted two sticks from the fire and handed one to Eagle. A fist-sized chunk of meat sizzled pleasantly and dripped melting fat, as the injured young man suddenly realized that he was ravenously hungry.

"Eat!" said his host. He squatted on his heels and took a gigantic bite from his own stick.

CHAPTER 5

Eagle watched the other man as they ate, trying to learn more about him. He was still puzzled. There were things here which did not seem logical.

First was the stranger's flawless use of the tongue of the People. That would imply that this had been his tribe. Yet Eagle could remember no one who had been cast out in recent years. The last had been the renegade Badger, when Eagle had been too young to remember. It had been such an event, however, that Eagle had heard the story retold throughout all his life. Scarcely once in a generation would such a thing happen. Surely, an event of this striking import would be well-known in the tribe. Why had Eagle never heard of the man?

A brief thought crossed his mind that perhaps this might be Badger himself. But, no, the renegade had been killed by the Head Splitters, in full view of hundreds of the People. This outcast must have been wandering much longer, anyway.

Eagle looked more closely. If this man had been wandering more than twenty winters, he must be very old. The younger man tried to estimate his age but found it difficult. The stranger's hair was long, unbraided, and as black and shiny as the wing of a crow. His face, on the other hand, was deeply wrinkled, crisscrossed by the lines of many seasons in the sun and the wind. The nose was large, above a great slash of a mouth, almost absurdly ugly.

Eagle's curious gaze met the dark glance of the other, and he dropped his eyes. It would be as impolite to stare as to ask questions about the status of the outcast.

The gnawing question remained. How had the old man—Eagle had decided he must be very old—how had he survived the many years as a solitary recluse? One would think it would be only a short while until a lone outcast was discovered by some roving band of an enemy tribe. The Head Splitters would like nothing better than to capture and torture, kill, or enslave a warrior of the People. This old man must be the most clever strategist on the prairie to have avoided death or capture.

There was one other possibility, Eagle realized with a start. The man might be mad. If he were possessed of evil spirits, it would be extremely dangerous to kill him. The spirits would quickly enter into the nearest person available. Thus it would be prudent for any Head Splitter chancing on the recluse to avoid him if he appeared mad. Ah, might that not be the secret? A clever outcast might *appear* mad by careful planning. True, he seemed perfectly sane at this time, except for his outlandish appearance.

Beyond the strange manner of not cutting or braiding his hair, the old man did appear eccentric in other ways. His garments were of skins. Not well-tanned buckskins, carefully fitted after the manner of the People, but ragged, poorly handled skins with the fur still attached. His main body garment, whatever it might be called, was a shapeless rag which seemed to be made of coyote or wolf skins. It was belted carelessly around his lanky frame with a greasy thong at the waist.

His large feet were covered with clumsily contrived footwear, which may have been poorly tanned buffalo hide. Eagle saw with surprise that the two did not match. They were made of entirely different skins.

A robe which lay tossed carelessly across a nearby log presented an even stranger appearance. It was an uneven patchwork of several skins. Eagle recognized wolf, buffalo calf, antelope, and what may have been elk.

It seemed that the old man was either incredibly sloppy and

careless about his appearance or had gone to great pains to appear so. If the effort was deliberate, reflected Eagle, the recluse had certainly succeeded in his purpose. The general effect was easily that of a half-crazed, if not totally mad, individual.

Eagle decided that the old man had originally been of the People. In keeping with his outcast status, he had eliminated any custom or manner of dress that would reveal his origin. It had not been mandatory but might be chosen by the individual for reasons of his own.

Feeling somewhat better after another chunk of well-browned meat, Eagle attempted further conversation. He could ask a few questions without being considered impolite.

"I am Eagle," he began. "How are you called?"

The other stared at him again for a moment, then finally shrugged carelessly.

"I am the Old Man."

Strange, thought Eagle. Surely everyone has a name. And if this ragged recluse is called the Old Man, by whom is he called that?

Then another thought occurred to him, recalled from his childhood. There was the legendary character, the Trickster, subject of many tales around the lodge fires. This supernatural being had been present at creation, maybe before. He was called by many names in many tribes, but to the People he was sometimes called the Old Man of the Shadows. Had this strange-acting old outcast, wandering the prairie for many seasons, come to believe that he was actually the legendary Trickster? Perhaps he was crazier than he appeared. True, he had said only "the Old Man," but Eagle resolved to watch him closely for possibly dangerous behavior.

"And where is your lodge, Uncle?" Eagle again used the term of respect accorded any adult male of the People.

"My lodge is everywhere," the old man replied with a vague

sweeping gesture. "See, there is the smoke hole!" He pointed straight up and laughed, a harsh cackling sound.

Eagle was certain now. The old man was quite mad. Beyond that, he was unsure, and was becoming tired and irritable from his exertion and the constant pain in the injured leg. He must rest.

"You must rest now." The voice of the Old Man echoed his thoughts. "Here, lie down!"

With a swirl, he spread the patchwork skin robe on a level spot and stepped over to help Eagle struggle to his feet. The man was very tall and thin, Eagle now noticed, nearly a head taller than himself. And Eagle had always been considered tall among the People.

Gratefully, he sank down upon the robe and stretched his aching body at full length before the fire. The Old Man straightened his long frame and looked down for a moment.

"I go for more meat," he said simply. Then he was gone, with scarcely a sound in the loose gravel of the river bank.

Eagle awoke some time later to find Sun Boy overhead, the spotted light of his heavenly torch filtering through the sycamore leaves above. The fog was gone and the day warm and pleasant.

He turned his head to see that the fire had been built up again. The Old Man had returned and gone while Eagle slept. Beyond the fire a drying rack held strips of meat, and a curious jay cocked his head to look from a nearby branch. Eagle raised to one elbow to toss a pebble at the bird. One of his earliest memories was of a similar scene. He had been assigned to shoo birds and insects away from his mother's meat racks. Tall One had praised his diligence and had rewarded him with a treat, consisting of pounded hackberries mixed with melted buffalo suet and rolled into balls. He smiled at the memory. Strange, he had not thought of that for many years. Now his own son, Bobcat, was old enough to perform the function of guarding the drying meat.

A motion caught his eye, and Eagle turned quickly, to see the Old Man returning with another loin of buffalo. He dumped the fresh meat on a piece of hide spread near the rack and squatted to use his flint knife. His long ungainly legs reminded Eagle of a giant grasshopper hunched over the pile of meat. The Old Man's motions were swift and sure, however. He stripped thin slices from the loin and draped them over the sticks of the drying rack.

Suddenly the Old Man seemed to remember the presence of Eagle. He turned quickly, the piercing stare boring through the young man as before.

"Here. You cut meat!"

He tossed a large, shapeless chunk at the young man, who barely managed to catch it to keep it from falling in the dirt. Again, Eagle was irritated. It was not that he objected to performing the chore. Though it was basically women's work, men of the People often participated in the preparation of meat after a hunt. The objectionable thing was the tone of command, the patronizing, demeaning attitude, hard to explain. Hard to understand, even.

Still irritated, Eagle grimly sliced thin strips and laid them aside to hang on the drying frame.

CHAPTER 6

Eagle would remember the next few days for the rest of his life. There was a muddled blend of sleep and awakening, with the constant underlying pain whenever he tried to move. He had used up all his extra strength, that superhuman reserve which becomes available for temporary use in extreme emergency. Now the letdown was profound.

He found himself weak as a newborn calf, his thoughts were confused, and his brief intervals of sleep were restless, filled with troubled dreams. In many of the vague, unformed visions, he was again riding a runaway horse among countless buffalo, across an unending world heavy with fog. He relived the sensation of falling, as his elk-dog was forced over the bluff. Then he would awake with a startled cry, sweat lying cold on his brow and across his shoulders.

Sometimes on awakening he would be alone, utterly alone in all of the prairie. The only sounds were bird songs or the chatter of a squirrel in the trees along the river. On other occasions he would wake to find the strange old man standing and staring at him quietly.

Eagle was still uneasy about the man's intentions and made more so by his quiet comings and goings. Sometimes it seemed that the ungainly feet of the Old Man made no noise at all, that he drifted as effortlessly as the fog along the river.

Once, Eagle's confused visions included the Old Man. He had once again heard in his dream the thunder of the stampeding buffalo and relived the terror of the fall from the bluff. Usually that was the event that awakened him, but this time he continued to dream. Somehow he was outside his body now, observing the scene with detached interest. He saw himself kick free of the falling horse, strike a glancing blow against the body of a struggling buffalo, and plunge into the stream. There he floated, face down, unconscious. Without emotion except that of curiosity, Eagle observed that he would quickly drown.

Then, from the bushes on the opposite shore strode a lanky figure, which Eagle recognized immediately as the Old Man. Only a few long steps took the stranger across the shallow part of the riffle, and he strode into the deeper pool without pause, plunging in up to his waist, then his armpits, before he reached the floating body. Eagle, in his observer's role, saw the scene in great detail. He could even see the texture of the loose strands of the Old Man's unbraided hair as it floated behind on the water.

Casually, almost carelessly, the tall man grasped the buckskin shirt of the unconscious figure and turned to wade out of the river. He strode up, out of the deeper water, dragging Eagle along by the nape of the neck, as a coyote drags her pup. Behind them, the crush of massive bodies continued to plunge over the bluff to destruction, piling up in the area just vacated. Scarcely looking backward, the ungainly figure continued to drag the limp form across the riffle and out onto the bank. There he simply let go, and Eagle's body slumped, half in and half out of the water near the top of the projecting strip of gravel. The Old Man quickly disappeared into the bushes.

Eagle, startled, realized that this was the exact spot and position in which he had been when he had awakened. The shock of the experience roused him, and the dream was gone. He woke suddenly, sitting upright in alarm and glancing quickly around. There, sitting beyond the fire, was the Old Man. He was solemnly staring, boring through with unfathomable dark eyes that seemed to see and know all.

Damp with cold sweat, Eagle sank back, exhausted and

trembling. What did it mean? Was this how he had escaped death at the bluff? But how had he been permitted to relive it as an observer in his own dream? Of one thing he was certain. The Old Man knew much more of this than he pretended.

As he calmed down and was able to control his trembling, Eagle felt an illogical anger at the Old Man. Why would the other behave in such secretive, mysterious ways? Eagle had always been a straightforward, open person. He had no time for fathoming of mysteries. It was his way to meet a situation head-on, directly, with no subterfuge. Even his brother Owl sometimes angered him with his thoughtful, mystical attitude. Of course, it was Owl's way, as a medicine man.

Perhaps this gangling stranger was a medicine man. But, no, he appeared to possess none of the medicine bags, pouches, and trappings of a medicine man.

Eagle was now in control of his trembling and weakness, and nearly over the flush of irritation at the other.

"Uncle," he asked calmly, "did you pull me from the river?"

The reply was irritating beyond measure. The ungainly old man merely shrugged, a noncommittal, careless movement of the shoulders, as if it were a matter of extreme unimportance.

"I drag many things from the river," he mused.

His vast mouth spread in what was intended for a smile, exposing irregular, yellowed teeth. He chuckled mirthlessly to himself.

Crazy, thought Eagle. Completely, totally mad! If he had dragged the unconscious form from the water, the Old Man had probably forgotten it by now.

Another thought struck the frustrated Eagle. Suppose the Old Man had been the means of his escape from drowning or being crushed. If the lanky outcast had been willing to go to the effort to save his life, why had he not ministered to the young man's injuries? Could the strange old man be so demented that he had merely pulled the limp Eagle ashore and then forgotten what he was doing, in midstride? Such things could happen to those possessed, Eagle thought. He would ask Owl sometime.

Feeling somewhat better, recovered from his frightening dream and now fully awake, Eagle glanced at the Old Man again.

"Is there any meat?"

"Yes."

The gangling oldster carelessly jerked a gnarled thumb at the fire without looking.

Frustrated, Eagle exhaled audibly, but the other seemed not to notice. It would take so little effort, Eagle fumed to himself, for the man to hand him some food. Instead, the Old Man sat, nonchalantly picking his teeth with a twig. Obviously, he had already eaten.

Eagle resolved to ask the man for nothing. He looked toward the fire and saw a succulent slab of buffalo meat, propped with sticks near the coals. It appeared cooked to perfection. Painfully, he rolled over and rose to his hands and his uninjured knee. He could crawl the few steps to reach his food.

The process was slow and painful, the most movement he had attempted since the first day, three suns ago. Once, tired and with the leg throbbing, Eagle was tempted to stop and ask for help. Perhaps he would have, but at that moment the Old Man opened his ample mouth and belched loudly. It was an echoing rumble of such proportions that Eagle was first startled, then irritated.

Could the man be so completely indifferent to his suffering that he did not even notice? Eagle shot another quick glance at the Old Man. Now the other was sprawled on his back in the sun, absently scratching his crotch. Eagle gritted his teeth in pain and anger and continued to crawl.

When he finally reached the fire, Eagle sank to a sitting position and reached for the meat. He tore loose a mouthful and began to chew. The taste was pleasant, and he looked across at the Old Man with a feeling of self-satisfaction.

However, the other seemed completely oblivious. He was gazing off at the sky, a dreamy smile on his rawboned face. He hummed, half to himself, some senseless little song.

Mad, thought Eagle again. Completely possessed.

CHAPTER 7

The weather continued warm and pleasant, and the two unlikely companions settled into a sort of routine.

Eagle found that he could begin to move around the camp
area. With the aid of a stout stick to lean on, he could hobble
a few steps for firewood or water, or to replenish the supply of
meat at the fire. He was still very careful not to put any
weight on the injured leg, but now rested it more easily on the
ground.

The Old Man seemed content to let Eagle do all he would.
It continued to be a sore point with the younger man. Sometimes it would have been so easy for the Old Man merely to
hand something or do some slight task himself. Instead, he
was more likely to lie half-sleeping or basking in the sunlight,
belching, scratching, or breaking wind, oblivious to Eagle's
efforts.

They worked together to some extent, Eagle helping to slice
and dry great amounts of the buffalo meat. There was plenty
available, in the dozens of carcasses strewn for a hundred
paces along the base of the bluff. It was necessary to process
what meat they could before decomposition set in. Already,
the sickly sweet smell of death and decay was beginning to
drift across the river.

One doubt increasingly gnawed at Eagle's mind, however.
Was the Old Man using him? It appeared that the oldster had
seen the opportunity to lay in his winter's food supply with the
help of his injured companion.

Each time the gangling figure ambled back from the river

with another armful of dripping meat to slice and dry, Eagle became more and more irritated. Before long, he became unsure as to just which irritated him more. Was it the intermittent work or the periods of inactivity in which the Old Man indulged in his repulsive personal habits?

Perhaps worst of all was the Old Man's snoring. The first time it occurred, Eagle sat up in fright, in the darkness of their first night together. The sound was a raucous, rattling roar, like a mixture of a rutting bull's bellow and the booming screech of the green night heron. The huge, cavernous nose seemed to amplify the sound, trumpeting forth the clarion call until the sycamore leaves overhead quivered. Irritably, Eagle tossed a stick at the sleeper, who turned on his side, murmured aloud, and lapsed back into sleep.

Eagle, at times, was ready to accept the theory that everything the Old Man did was an attempt to make the younger man uncomfortable or irritated.

True, he was sometimes helpful, Eagle had to admit. He had brought food when Eagle was unable to acquire his own. He had lent his own outlandish cape for Eagle's bed the first day. Later, he had brought a ragged, freshly skinned buffalo hide for the injured youth. It proved more comfortable for sleeping than the Old Man's cape and even more so after the buffalo lice had moved on.

Fortunately for Eagle's peace of mind, the Old Man spent much time off wandering somewhere. Eagle attempted to ask a time or two about the activities of the other. He received only a noncommittal shrug and gave up trying to find out. He decided to be merely grateful for time spent apart.

He had decided that the Old Man must have some sort of a winter lodge or shelter, probably nearby. Bundles of dried buffalo meat continually vanished as they were completed, though Eagle rarely saw the Old Man remove them. Surely he must be carrying the supplies off for storage. Again Eagle was irritated at the secretive behavior of the other.

One afternoon, in the absence of the Old Man, Eagle experienced a sobering event. He was drowsing in the mottled sunshine under the trees when a flash of motion caught his eye. Instantly he was alert, scanning the distant slope. Over a low, grassy ridge a few hundred paces away rode a single file of horsemen.

His first thought was of the fire, but a quick glance told him it was low and without smoke. Next he rolled quickly behind a thin screen of brush, to observe unseen until the newcomers were identified.

Cautiously, Eagle peered between the fronds of the dogwood thicket. The riders were nearer now, and by their dress and weapons he could discern the worst. Here was a party of twenty warriors, well armed. They carried lances, bows, and shields, and from each waist dangled a heavy stone war club. This was no hunting party but a war party of the enemy, the dreaded Head Splitters.

They paused on the distant slope, talking and gesturing. Eagle gathered that they were pointing at a couple of circling buzzards, asking each other why the birds were attracted to the area of the river bluff. Then, to the utter consternation of the hidden Eagle, the leader turned his horse and started almost directly toward the campsite.

Eagle slid quietly into a more dense thicket of brush, knowing that the effort was useless. If the enemy discovered the camp, they would scatter and search until they found him. They would have at least one skilled tracker. In a matter of moments, they would read in the signs that two men camped here and that one was injured or crippled.

At least, Eagle told himself wryly, they would have great difficulty identifying this as a camp of the People. The nondescript junk that comprised the belongings of the Old Man bore no identifying characteristics.

The riders moved closer, the horses picking their way

among the loose white scatter of stone on the hillside. A thin strip of blood-red sumac stretched across the meadow. Eagle watched, fascinated, as the leader threaded his way into the fringe of sumac, twisting and turning to avoid the gnarled twigs. Scarlet leaves, ripe already, shattered at the touch of his passing and fluttered to the ground.

Suddenly the elk-dog reared and plunged, nearly falling backward. The startled rider, caught off balance, fell heavily over the animal's rump and landed on his head and shoulders. Almost instantly the warrior was rolling, however, frantically clawing his way backward. The horse lunged aside to run wildly back up the slope, running blindly, shaking its head as if to escape something clinging to its face. The other warriors scattered, retreating back the way they had come, their horses stumbling among the loose stones of the hillside.

And, to Eagle's amazement, the warriors were laughing! They shouted to each other and pointed to the unhorsed warrior, still scrambling in the grass. The astonished Eagle had a momentary thought that by some unknown means, some very strong medicine, the enemy had been caused to go mad.

In a moment, however, he saw the cause for all the consternation and hilarity. A small black-and-white animal shuffled deliberately into the open from a clump of plume grass. Its fluffy tail held high, the creature swung its rump toward the retreating group, stamping hind feet threateningly.

Eagle nearly laughed aloud with delight. He would tell this story for the rest of his life, of watching an entire war party of the Head Splitters routed by one small smell-cat. Apparently the leader's horse had nearly stepped on the creature and had received most of the noxious spray directly in the face and eyes. Strong medicine, indeed!

By the time the warriors recovered from their disorganization and captured the runaway horse, they had apparently forgotten their intention to explore the river. They straggled downstream, still laughing and talking, well upwind from their discomfited leader. That warrior rode alone, angry and sullen, probably very sore from the fall as well as strong-smelling.

The enemy party moved out of sight, and partially Eagle began to relax. He was concerned for the Old Man, for there was no way to know where that individual might be. Though Eagle was perpetually irritated, he had no desire to have the Old Man meet an untimely end at the hands of a party of Head Splitters.

He crawled back to the campsite and waited. It seemed a long time, and the buzzards had drawn many circles in the cloudless sky before the Old Man ambled in across the meadow. He was humming some senseless little song to himself, completely oblivious of everything. Eagle felt the old twinge of resentment and irritation.

"Did you see the Head Splitters?" he asked.

Slowly the Old Man looked around.

"Where? I see no Head Splitters."

"You saw none? A war party, fully armed?"

"Of course not! Eagle, you are dreaming again!"

Frustrated, Eagle sat against the sycamore tree. Could he possibly have dreamed the entire scene? But, no, it *was* real. He had not been sleeping. He would say no more, he thought, but he was certain. He had had a very narrow escape from death or capture by the Head Splitters. It did not matter whether the crazy old man believed him or not.

The Old Man moved around the camp, building up the fire, while Eagle sat, angry and frustrated. A stray puff of breeze floated past, carrying the mixed scents of the Old Man's body and his motley furs. But there was something else.

Just for a moment, as the ungainly figure passed, Eagle caught a trace of another scent. There was no mistake. Mingled with the odors of campfire smoke, drying meat, sweat, and furs was another, a musky, animal scent. There could be no other like it. It was the distinct odor of the smell-cat.

Now Eagle was more frustrated than ever. The actions of the Old Man became more and more mysterious. The oldster must have been near enough to the action in the meadow to have been anointed with the smell-cat's spray. How had he avoided detection?

More importantly, why had he lied about it?

CHAPTER 8

By the next day, Eagle was not so certain about the entire episode in the meadow. Possibly the Old Man had encountered a different smell-cat. It could even have occurred that he had picked up a hint of the scent merely by walking through the grass and sumac in the meadow where the smell-cat had sprayed.

"Did you see a smell-cat?" Eagle finally asked in frustration.

The old man looked sharply at him, almost suspiciously.

"Of course! There are many smell-cats."

True, thought Eagle, but the matter was not really one of smell-cats. It was that in the entire period of time they had been together, he had asked many questions of the Old Man, but received not a single direct answer. Why must the man be so evasive, so devious, about such simple things as smell-cats? He resolved to watch the Old Man closely, to try to catch him in an inconsistency.

This proved more difficult than Eagle imagined. He had already noticed how quietly the other moved. The Old Man seemed to be able to cross the noisy clattering gravel of the bar at the river without dislodging a stone. Then, at times, the oldster appeared from a direction entirely different from that Eagle expected. All the comings and goings of the Old Man seemed shrouded in mystery. And where could he be taking all the dried meat?

Then there was the episode of the heron. Eagle awoke just as Sun Boy was lighting his torch. The steam was lifting from the warm surface of the river, to mingle with the cooler air of the morning. To an observer a few paces away and at ground level, the river appeared to smolder, with the smoke of a hundred dying campfires rising to become the fog of the morning.

As Eagle rubbed sleep from his eyes, he looked around for the Old Man. At first, he did not see the other at all. Then a puff of breeze parted the wisps of fog, and Eagle saw the lanky form at the river.

The Old Man was standing motionless, as he sometimes did, frozen in an odd position. He was at the very edge of the water, maybe even standing in the shallows of the riffle. He balanced on one leg, the other drawn up under him, with the foot resting on his bony kneecap. His arms were folded casually, and his head cocked to one side, absently looking and listening to the morning. The odd angle made the large nose appear even larger, longer, and sharper, as the shifting light and shadow of the morning fluttered across the motionless scene.

Drifting wisps of fog obscured Eagle's vision for a moment, and he rolled over to rise for the day. He picked up a few sticks to toss on the remaining embers of the night's fire and experienced irritation that the Old Man had not seen to that task. Why, when the other had been the first to rise, had he not seen to such simple things as tending the fire? Resentfully, Eagle glanced again toward the river.

The scene was unchanged. There was the soft sound of water murmuring quietly across the riffle and the distant call of a jay. The fog still lifted from the smooth surface of the water, partially obscuring the shapes of trees, rocks, and the heavy shadow of the bluff on the opposite bank. The ungainly shape of the Old Man could be seen dimly through the shifting mists. Then the vapors thinned for a moment, and Eagle was able to see the other very plainly.

To his astonishment, the figure at the water's edge was not the Old Man at all. A great blue heron stood on one leg in the shallows, the other foot folded under it. The bird's head was cocked to one side, watching, listening for any small water creature that might provide a meal. Its long sharp beak was poised at an awkward angle, but ready to thrust instantly at an unwary fish or frog.

Eagle watched the bird, wondering how he could have been deceived in his first observation. In a moment the creature seemed to feel his gaze and uncomfortably shifted to look directly at him. For the space of a heartbeat, Eagle felt the bright eye of the heron upon him and felt oddly as he did when the dark glance of the Old Man bored into his consciousness.

Then, without warning and before Eagle had recovered from his momentary confusion, the heron flew. Majestically, noiselessly, the great wings spread and lifted the creature into the air. Ungainly and almost ugly when standing or walking, the bird now became a thing of complete grace and beauty. The broad wings, stretching wider than the span of a man's outstretched arms, drew the heron upward at each stroke.

The rays of Sun Boy's torch struck the soft blue-gray color of the bird's feathers as it lifted above the shadows of the river and into full sunlight. Eagle stood, fascinated, feeling for a moment as if he, too, could lift above the fog and fly, up from the shadows of crippled existence, restrained by an injured leg. Then the bird was gone, and Eagle stood alone.

Now puzzling questions came pouring at him again. How had he been deceived into thinking that the heron, wading the shadows to look for fish, could possibly resemble the Old Man? Eagle shook his head in irritation at himself and turned again to the fire.

By the time the Old Man returned, across the meadow from the south, Eagle believed that his mind had been playing tricks on him. It was logical, as he awoke, rubbing sleep from his eyes, to misinterpret things seen dimly through the mists of the morning. At least, that was the explanation he used as he tried to convince himself. The effort was not entirely successful.

Eagle was still unsatisfied when darkness came and he prepared for sleep. He had seen herons many times, had admired their hunting skill and their graceful flight, but this experience was different. In this simple scene there had been, somehow, something special. There was a sort of thrill, a feeling of *almost* understanding some important thing that now eluded him.

Perhaps it was this restless feeling that caused Eagle to dream. It was one of those times when, to himself, he appeared to be awake and aware that he was dreaming. Yet, at the same time, the dream seemed so real as he experienced it.

He was a child again, sitting at a story fire. There were other children there. Eagle's own brother, Owl, two summers younger, sat at his left.

The storyteller was Eagle's own grandfather, the Coyote. Of all the people who told stories to the young, Eagle enjoyed most the tales of Coyote. The paunchy little man could make a story come alive for the listener. Coyote was not a chief but was respected by all for his wisdom. The chiefs listened seriously when Coyote spoke in the council.

But best of all, for the young, were his stories. His lined face would be serious or smiling or sad, depending on the mood of the story, but his eyes were always bright and shining, excited with the thrill of the moment. Eagle loved to hear the throaty little chuckle for which Coyote was named. It was like the distant sound of the hunting animal calling to its mate.

On this occasion, in his dream, Eagle was listening to tales of the Old Man of the Shadows. Coyote had warned that stories of the Trickster must never be told except after darkness has fallen. Eagle was reexperiencing the thrill of excitement and a little fear. The children peered past the fire and into the patchy darkness of the brush along the creek and under the trees. The short hairs on the back of young Eagle's neck prickled with excitement. His brother scooted closer to him and glanced over his shoulder into the darkness.

Eagle was glad for the security of Owl's nearness. He would never have made such a move himself, but he was glad that Owl had done so.

The story, known so well from retelling since Eagle was old enough to remember, was about the bobcat. That animal's tail was short, as every child knew, because of a disagreement with the Trickster. The legendary figure, seeking revenge, had turned himself into a hollow tree. The Trickster, Coyote explained, could turn himself into any animal or bird he chose, even a tree or a rock. That could be very useful.

As if he were hearing the story for the first time, Eagle in his dream, was forming pictures in his mind. He could clearly imagine the bobcat, originally with a long tail like that of the real-cat, the cougar. He could see the Trickster himself, as described by Coyote. The Old Man of the Shadows was always the same in the stories. Tall, ungainly, with unbraided hair and a big nose. He dressed in skins.

The thoughts of Eagle's dream and those of that semiconscious part of him that realized it was a dream began to bump together, interrupting the smooth flow of sleep. Uneasily, Eagle struggled up toward the surface of consciousness in the real world. There was something he must try to remember. Something about the dream or about the story he had been listening to in the dream. Half-awake, he struggled to sort out that which was story, which was dream, and which was reality. He opened his eyes and sat up, and there was a moment when he felt a pang of regret that he was no longer really a child at his grandfather's knee.

It was moonlight, now. The Old Man lay snoring in his robe. Probably it was the raucous bellow of his snore that had awakened Eagle. The younger man turned on his side and pulled his own robe over his shoulder against the night's chill. He glanced back at the sleeper.

The Old Man's long unbraided hair fell across his arm and glistened in the moonlight. Watching him a moment, Eagle suddenly realized what it was that he had been trying to remember.

The description of the Old Man of the Shadows was basically unchanging, no matter who told the stories. It was in each listener's head to see how the Trickster might look. Eagle had had the picture in his head since he was small.

A few days ago, Eagle had wondered if this strange demented old man thought he was actually the Trickster. Now Eagle wondered something else. He had just realized what was bothering him.

How did it happen that the Old Man's appearance so nearly resembled Eagle's mind-pictures of the Old Man of the Shadows?

CHAPTER 9

During the bright light of day, Eagle determined to attempt once more to question the Old Man. He was still troubled by the recurring ideas that kept coming back in his mind. Disturbing ideas, thoughts which brought memories of childhood tales of the Trickster. By daylight, with the pungent scents of the Moon of Ripening pleasant to the senses, his thoughts of the night seemed ridiculous.

Eagle glanced over at the Old Man, dozing in the sun and sleepily brushing at a fly on his nose. They had eaten, the other had belched loudly and immediately reclined for a nap. How could Eagle have been reminded of the legendary Trickster by this simple, almost repulsive old outcast?

He waited impatiently until his companion awoke, yawned, belched, scratched himself, and nodded to him in recognition. Then he cautiously approached the subject.

"Uncle, do you remember the stories of the Trickster?"

The reaction was immediate and spectacular. The Old Man whirled in anger, glaring at his questioner.

"Why do you ask me that?"

Without waiting, he hurried on.

"You know these things must never be mentioned except in the time of darkness!"

Still irritated, he wheeled and strode away through the trees, gesturing and talking to himself. He did not return.

Meanwhile, Eagle had time alone to think. He determined not to mention the subject of the Trickster again. For whatever reason, the Old Man's rage had been a frightening thing. Eagle had no desire to see a recurrence of the scene.

The afternoon dragged on, the shadows cast by Sun Boy's torch lengthened, and the muted gray blue of the prairie twilight settled like a soft robe thrown over the plains.

The night passed slowly. Eagle had not slept, uneasy and anxious over the Old Man's reaction. Was it possible that he had gone for good, leaving the injured Eagle to fend for himself? This gnawing doubt alone would have kept Eagle from sleep. He realized just how much he had come to depend on the strange old man. Had he now, by a stupid question, destroyed the only hope for survival that he seemed to have?

Eagle lay troubled on his robe, watching the stars wheel slowly around the Real-star in the north. He watched the Seven Hunters until they dipped below the rim of the river's bluff. A night bird called somewhere, and from some distance downstream came the hollow call of *kookooskoos*, the great owl. A fish jumped, making a tinkling splash in the smooth surface of the river.

It was well past the halfway point of the time of darkness before the Old Man shuffled into the dim circle of firelight. He grunted a sound that might be taken for a greeting and spread his robe to sleep. Then, just before he lapsed into his pattern of obnoxious snoring, the lanky figure raised to an elbow and spoke quietly.

"Eagle, we must move tomorrow. The rains come."

The younger man had had such thoughts himself. He had, in fact, mentioned it a time or two but failed to receive a direct answer.

Actually, their camp was in a very vulnerable location. The fine weather of the Moon of Ripening had made Eagle feel too secure. Long, warm afternoons, the smell and feel of autumn, were disarming. It was pleasant to sit and feel the sun on one's body, to watch the long lines of geese honking their way south across the sky. Much more pleasant than to worry about the coming onslaught of Cold Maker from the north.

He had avoided the responsibility for decision. He had allowed the Old Man to influence him, since the oldster seemed to be making all the decisions anyway. It was easier merely to go along.

Even so, Eagle had begun to be concerned about the Old Man's apparent lack of direction. Certain conditions were becoming almost intolerable. When the usual south breezes occasionally swung to the north, the stench of rotting buffalo carcasses was nearly overwhelming. The Old Man seemed not to notice and, when Eagle mentioned it, merely shrugged. They had long since given up all attempts to salvage any more of the meat. They had abandoned the remainder to the buzzards, coyotes, and other scavengers, whose activities continued day and night.

The most dangerous aspect of their situation, however, was the camp's location on the low bank of the river. A rise in the river's level of only little more than a hand's span would put their camp in water.

At some time, as the Moon of Ripening changed to the Moon of Falling Leaves, there would be rain. It was easy for Eagle to put that aside in his mind. In the warm hazy afternoons the threat of expected rain seemed remote and unlikely, and it was much more comfortable to remain inactive. The injured leg still pained considerably when he moved. Yet, he realized that whether he thought about it or not, the rains would come. Before that time, they must move the camp.

Eagle still suspected that, in spite of his vague denial, the Old Man actually had a well-provisioned winter lodge somewhere. Whether he would condescend to share that shelter with the injured Eagle was another question.

The young man waited until he felt that his surly companion was in a comparatively good humor and initiated a conversation once again.

"Uncle," he began tentatively, "you said last night that we must move."

The Old Man only grunted, but nodded an indifferent affirmative and continued to gnaw on the food he was eating.

"Where, Uncle?"

The dark eyes bored into Eagle's for a moment, then softened somewhat. The Old Man turned slowly, to gaze at the face of the bluff opposite. There was a long silence as he seemed to study the fissured rock. Finally, it seemed almost at random, he carelessly poked a gnarled finger at the cliff.

"There."

"Beyond the bluff?"

"Of course not. *In* it."

"*In* it? A cave, Uncle?"

Again, the frustrating shrug, the nonanswering grunt that could mean anything. Irritated, Eagle lapsed into silence, realizing that the conversation was terminated, at least from the Old Man's viewpoint.

Quietly, he lay propped on an elbow and studied the rocky face opposite them. It appeared a cracked and fissured wall of gray-white stone, discolored in places with patches of moss and lichens of unpredictable hues. In the larger crevices, small trees had found a foothold, and here and there smaller defects supported straggly growths of plum, dogwood, and thorn berry. Try as he would, Eagle could see no path up the face of the cliff. He searched the entire portion that was visible to him, little by little. From the point downstream where the bend of the river hid the bluff from further view, to the indistinct blur of distance upstream, he could detect no definite means of ascent.

There were several irregularities in the rock that could have represented the entrances to small caves. None could be seen with clarity, and as Eagle watched, he realized that the shifting of light and shadow presented an ever-changing appearance. It was impossible to discern any definite location for the cave mentioned by the Old Man.

Then, through his irritation at the other's reluctance to give him any information at all came another doubt. Suppose, Eagle pondered, suppose there is a cave and a trail or path up to it. How could he, with a badly injured leg, possibly reach the shelter? He could barely move the few steps around the campfire to attend to his bodily needs. Did the Old Man imagine that somehow Eagle could climb that sheer cliff?

Annoyed and frustrated, Eagle watched the Old Man gather up his odds and ends of nondescript personal possessions. The Old Man made a sort of pack from his multiskinned robe, loosely wrapping his fire sticks, a knife, and a gourd rattle with some odd pieces of furs. Eagle had noticed the rattle before but had never seen the Old Man use it. It was quite plain, adorned with only one simple medicine symbol, one which was unfamiliar to Eagle. And, of course, one did not ask about another's medicine.

The Old Man picked up the shapeless pack and swung it to his bony shoulders. Without a word, he strode off among the trees.

Eagle experienced the anxious moment of doubt which he always did when the Old Man left the camp but with more impact. Would he return? The young man's extreme helplessness had been made clear to him by the close call when the enemy war party had passed.

Now, the other had departed without comment, taking all his possessions, everything in the camp except the makeshift robe on which Eagle lay and the buckskins the young man wore. Uneasily, Eagle felt for the knife at his waist. At least, it was there.

"Uncle?" he called anxiously after the retreating figure.

There was no answer except the distant chatter of a squirrel in the trees along the river.

CHAPTER 10

Eagle sat, disturbed, for a time, waiting for the Old Man's return. Sun Boy traveled across the arch of the sky and started back toward his lodge on the Other Side, as Eagle became more and more alarmed. This time, he felt, the Old Man had really departed for good.

Anger welled up in him, resentment and fury at the crazy old outcast. To have befriended a helpless and injured man, to entice him to help prepare a winter's food supply and then leave him helpless and alone, was unforgivable.

Eagle's sullen thoughts were interrupted by a rustle in the dry growth of tallgrass on the slope across the meadow. It was only a few heartbeats until he became aware of the cause. The wind was shifting. What had been a warm, balmy puff of south breeze on his cheek had now changed. For a short while there had been quiet in the movement of the air. It was so subtle that Eagle had failed to notice that the breeze had calmed.

Then had come the change. Twisting, nipping, and whirling came the shifting wind puffs from the north, stirring not only the grasses opposite now but the treetops above him. Anxiously, Eagle turned to look to the northwest.

Just above the rim of the river's bluff lay an ugly, puffy bank of dark gray-blue clouds. Streaks of real-fire darted within the cloud bank, and Eagle heard the distant mutter, the accompanying thunder of Rain Maker's dance drum.

He must move at once. Quickly he glanced around, evaluated the closest high ground. It was straight across the meadow, through the fringe of sumac, and up the opposite slope. Several hundred paces it would be, and that only to the foot of the slope. Then he would have to look for shelter, but for now it was essential that he move, and rapidly. Rain Maker's drum boomed again.

Quickly, Eagle threw his skin robe around his shoulders. He looked for a moment at the fire. Perhaps he should take a burning brand and a supply of dry wood. He realized how limited would be his ability to carry anything. He must bear his full weight on his good leg and the pole he had fashioned. This would leave only one hand free.

Again, he looked toward the cloud bank. *Aiee!* How fast it grew now. Eagle snatched a handful of dry twigs and a couple of burning sticks from the fire. He grasped his pole and set out across the meadow.

For the first few steps, Eagle felt that he was doing well. Then he began to tire rapidly, his breath coming in hoarse gasps. His grip weakened on the staff, and he slipped.

Eagle was aware of the importance of his injured leg. He must, at all costs, avoid further injury to it. Therefore, to protect the leg, he allowed himself to fall. He attempted to roll, but fell clumsily, landing with a jarring impact that forced the air from his body with an audible grunt.

As he lay, trying to catch his breath, he turned to look toward his goal. The slope seemed so far away in his weakened state. It must be a few hundred steps, but each step would be agony. He must not panic. He would take only a few steps at a time, then rest. There would be plenty of time before the river rose to flood the meadow. At least that was his hope. He struggled to an erect position and lurched ahead.

It was at his second rest stop that the first fat drops of rain struck. Anxiously, Eagle glanced around. The trees along the river appeared strangely different from this angle, the gray bluff rising high behind them. Even as he looked, the driving rush of the storm whipped across the river, the twisting winds lashing tormented trees for a few moments before the entire scene was obliterated in the driving rain.

Eagle turned to look the other way. He was far less than halfway to the slope. Then, that view was also obscured as the leading edge of the rain washed over and past him. He gasped at how cold the deluge became. Surely Cold Maker had joined his brother for this onslaught.

Teeth chattering, he started on. He knew that it must be near dark. Sun Boy had already been low when Eagle first noticed the approach of the storm.

He realized that he was still holding a sodden handful of wet sticks, now useless for the fire he had hoped to build. He tossed them aside.

Now he could grasp his staff with both hands, but it helped little. Eagle could take only a few steps before he must stop, exhausted, drawing breath in ragged gasps. He would despair of reaching the slope, then catch his breath and plunge forward again, struggling ahead.

Eagle was not precisely aware, in the deepening darkness, when the river began to rise. He was so wet, so chilled, that he was unsure of the moment when the wetness of his already wet moccasins became the wetness of wading through water on the ground. The only immediate difference was that the water of the rising river seemed a trifle warmer than that pouring from the sky. Then even that difference was gone.

Eagle struggled forward, trembling and chilled to the bone, hoping to reach the broken rocks at the opposite rim. Perhaps he could find some protection in the shelter of a sun-warmed rock. The great blocks of stone should retain enough of Sun Boy's heat to assist in survival.

It was full dark now, and the only illumination was from the occasional flash that penetrated the driving rain. Rain Maker threw a bolt of real-fire against a large cottonwood tree near the top of the slope. For an instant it was illuminated from top to bottom, and then all was blackness again. Eagle still saw the outline of the stricken tree, burned orange and green into his sight, even when he closed his eyes. He blinked to clear his vision and sat down in the shallow water.

Another flash of lightning showed the slope ahead, nearer now and yet so far. He rose and struggled on. He had no clear idea how high the water might rise or how far it would be necessary to go.

Once more, he slipped and fell, once more twisting, taking a hard, painful, jarring impact to avoid landing on the injured leg. Still, the shock sent stabbing pains up the leg, racing upward to smash against the base of his skull. He doubted if he could manage to avoid injury the next time he fell.

His movements were slower now. He rolled over to try to regain his feet, wallowing in the chilling water. He groped for his staff, failed to find it, and sank back, beaten and dejected. For the first time in his life, Eagle, first son of Heads Off and Tall One, had reached the point where he acknowledged defeat. He could go no farther.

One last time he turned to look in the direction of the river and the bluff, the thing that had beaten him in the strength of his youth. Why, after all this delay? Why had he not been allowed to cross over immediately?

His thoughts softened with regret at the thought of his family. His wife, Sweet Grass, would find another husband. She was young, pretty, and everyone knew her to be a good wife. Someone would take her, perhaps his brother Owl.

Eagle regretted that he would not live to see his children grown. He was proud of them. The eldest, Bobcat, was a happy, well-formed child, intelligent enough to make a great warrior some day.

But the other, the girl. *Aiee*, there was one to be reckoned with. She was so intense, so direct and to the point. Her mind seemed to work like his own, which pleased him greatly. Already, people called her Little Eagle or sometimes Eagle Woman. This, too, pleased him.

A sudden crash of thunder split the sky, and by the light of the real-fire, Eagle saw a tall figure standing over him. Then all was darkness again.

"Why did you come this way?" the Old Man snapped irritably. "Not this way. That way!"

In the darkness, Eagle could not distinguish which way. He struggled to answer.

"I nearly could not find you!" the Old Man ranted on. "Here! Get up! Climb on my back!"

Eagle felt the firm grasp of a gnarled fist close around his wrist. Almost effortlessly, it seemed, he felt the Old Man pick him up and swing him like a sack of meat. Somehow, he landed astride the bony back.

"Hold on tight, no matter what happens!"

There was no denying the commanding tone of the Old Man's terse order. The next minute, Eagle could feel the Old Man running beneath him, bounding, leaping over obstacles, splashing through the shallow water. Numbly, Eagle wondered, How can he see where he is going?

CHAPTER 11

Eagle clung tightly to the Old Man's shoulders and gripped with his thighs to the best of his ability. His injured leg dangled, useless, but by keeping a sense of the rhythm of the runner's motion, he was able to hold on. After the first few moments, it became almost instinctive. Not unlike riding a horse, Eagle thought.

He had no idea which direction they were moving and did not care. His mind was numb from cold and exhaustion, and it was easier merely to close his eyes against the beating downpour of icy rain. Occasionally, he was startled by a flash of real-fire and opened his eyes for an instant of illumination, to see practically nothing. There was water everywhere, apparently shallow water, as the Old Man continued to run through it.

Somewhere ahead, and perhaps to the left, there was a vague sensation of heavy shape. It felt—yes, *felt*, because it could not be seen in the darkness—like the mass of the river's bluff. Eagle thought it odd that the Old Man would be running toward the angry, treacherous current of the rising river. To him, it still seemed they should be moving to higher ground, away from the flood. But there was little choice. He was too tired to wonder at such odd behavior just now.

The strange pair plunged into the timber, and there was a sudden calm as they were sheltered from the driving force of the wind. Rain still fell heavily, but it now fell or dropped from the trees above in a steady, sodden downpour. There was at least a partial relief from the lashing bite of wind-driven water in their faces.

Now the Old Man's gait slowed. They moved steadily forward, the oldster apparently feeling his way for solid footing among the rocks. Eagle's dangling foot, swinging uselessly with the movements of the Old Man, encountered the surface of the rising river. They were moving into deeper water!

Now, for the second time in a very short while, Eagle was ready to give himself up for dead. The strange old man must have gone completely crazy, carrying them directly into the rising torrent. The evil spirits within were driving him to destroy them both.

The situation infuriated Eagle. He had come so far, had suffered and overcome so much, and now to be drowned under circumstances which could have been avoided! The water reached his knees now.

"No," he screamed.

He pounded on the Old Man's head and shoulders, struggling to dismount. He would try to find a tree in the darkness, pull or drag himself up out of the torrent, somehow cling there until the flood subsided.

The Old Man slipped and almost fell. His arms grasped the legs of the struggling rider.

"Stop it! You must be still and hold on!"

There was urgency and command in the angry yell but something else, too. Somehow, there was a calm, solid reassurance, which penetrated Eagle's panic. He grasped the wet fur of the Old Man's skin garments and settled himself again. He felt like a child who has just been severely corrected. The Old Man stood still for a moment, waiting.

"Now," he said calmly and somewhat more gently, "put your arms around my neck. Hold tight. We are going across!"

Without further hesitation, he plunged forward again. In a step or two, the water was as deep as Eagle's groin, and his belly tightened against the shock. There was a quick intake of breath, a gasp. The first cold plunge always affected him that way. He grasped tightly around the Old Man's neck and grimly hung on.

Now the water had reached Eagle's chest, and he could feel that only the head of the Old Man was above the surface. Slowly, step by step, they moved forward, the lanky form braced against the current, feeling cautiously for footing.

Without warning they plunged beneath the surface. Eagle had only a heartbeat's span to realize that the Old Man had stepped into a hole, one of the treacherous deep places in the river's bed. Then he was gulping water instead of air, fighting to rise, frantically struggling upward. He knew he must not draw water into his lungs and could not avoid it. The worst, the most dreadful panic, was that he could not free himself from the floundering old man under him. He was unable to go longer without air, and still his legs were held tightly in the grasp of the other. Consciousness was slipping away.

Eagle could never quite remember exactly what happened after that. His semiconscious condition, the black darkness of the night, the panic of the river, all blended into a blur of terror that he would long dream about.

Somehow, in the midst of this moment of desperation, something happened. Beneath him, the gaunt body stiffened, the Old Man gave a sudden lunge, a surge of strength and power, and began to swim.

Eagle's head burst above the surface, sputtering and coughing. Now he instinctively realized that his only hope was to cling tightly to the Old Man. He stopped struggling to free himself and grasped for something to hold. Cold, numb fingers closed on the other's coarse hair, and still confused and desperate, Eagle hung on. The Old Man lunged forward, swimming strongly. In a moment, Eagle's instincts had adjusted to the changed rhythm of the swimmer's motion.

Again, he had the curious sensation that balancing on the lunging swimmer's back was much like riding a horse. Then his mind was playing tricks again. This night, with its blackness and terror, became mixed somehow with the experience of the stampede.

Eagle was riding again, as on the fateful day of the hunt. He saw again in his mind the endless world of buffalo, and in its midst, he was alone on a lunging elk-dog. Now the event was repeated. Instead of the buffeting by countless stampeding animals, he was now threatened by the rolling flood of the river. Instead of heat and dust there were wet and cold, instead of Sun Boy's light there was darkness, but the situation was the same. The only bit of reality in the unreal world was the firm sensation of the horse beneath him.

He grasped more tightly at the creature's mane and tightened his knees against the flanks. In his dreamlike state, the swimmer under him had become a mighty horse, confidently breasting the churning river. Every lunge, every snorting breath verified the impression.

Later, Eagle had been forced to admit that his senses that night were in no way acute enough to be relied on. At best, he was choking, fainting from exhaustion, chilled and half-drowned in the river. Still, it was so real at the time.

He remembered how it felt and sounded when the horse struck a rocky shelf and regained footing, scrambling up and onto the shore, while the rider clung tightly for life.

They stopped, and now there was no doubt about their location. The bulk of the bluff loomed above them, near enough to touch. They were on a narrow strip of bank, scarcely a pace or two wide, which lay between the bluff and the river. A brief flash verified this feeling.

Completely exhausted and unable to hold on any longer, Eagle slid from the wet hairy back of the horse and landed heavily on his side, still coughing water. More than anything, he wanted to rest, to lie here until he woke or died, it mattered little which.

"Get up."

With a foot, the Old Man nudged the prone form on the wet grass.

"Get up! We must climb!"

Eagle rolled halfway over and by the lightning's next flash saw the gaunt form standing over him. How could he have been so confused that he had thought there was a horse in the river? Ah, well, what did it matter?

"Climb? I cannot climb, Uncle."

The Old Man exhaled audibly, irritably.

"*Aiee*, you can do nothing!"

It was not so much a criticism as a statement of fact.

Gently, almost tenderly, he knelt and gathered the injured and exhausted Eagle in his arms, like a child. With long, confident strides, the Old Man started along the face of the bluff.

Eagle had a vague sensation that they were on a narrow path and that they were climbing, but he could never recall the entire ascent. He must have fallen asleep, cradled in the strong arms of the Old Man.

CHAPTER 12

Sun Boy carried his torch aloft next morning to light a wet, sodden world. The clouds had moved on, but there was a chill in the clean air that said Cold Maker would return.

Eagle awoke with the first light of day. He was warm, dry, and almost comfortable. It took a few moments to gather his thoughts and begin to think about where he might be. He remembered that there had been a storm, that he had nearly drowned in the flooding river. Uneasily, he remembered a confused episode when he had ridden a swimming horse across the deep water. The Old Man was involved. Had he been on the horse too? Eagle's memory of the entire time was very vague.

The Old Man had tried to get him to get up and climb, but Eagle had been unable to respond. Dimly, he remembered that he had been carried, that they had come to shelter of some sort. There, the Old Man had gently laid him down and thrown a robe over him.

Eagle turned his head to look around. He was in a sort of cave, lying on a bed made of skins thrown over some softer material, probably dried grasses such as the People used. A small fire burned in the center of the floor, and the smoke hovered against the stone arch overhead before gradually finding its way to a fissure leading upward. The blackened condition of the roof suggested many fires over a very long period of time.

The entire cave was perhaps three paces across. On the other side of the fire was a shapeless clutter of skins, which may have been another bed. The Old Man's odd multi-skinned robe was tossed carelessly across it, but the man himself was nowhere to be seen.

There was a dank, musty, animal odor about the cave, reminding Eagle of the smell of a bear's den or of the nests of mice behind the lining of a lodge.

As the light grew, Eagle could see more detail in the cave. There were some of the scanty personal possessions of the Old Man. He recognized the fire-making sticks and the gourd rattle. A willow rack supported a variety of bundles of various shapes and sizes. Eagle recognized some of the parcels as those of the dried meat he had helped to prepare.

At the end of the rack hung a small drum, decorated with the same strange symbols he had noted on the gourd rattle.

Beyond these simple things, the cave was empty. Eagle rolled over and looked toward the entrance. Blue sky was visible, with only a few fluffy clouds, high and distant. Most of the view, however, was obscured by a sturdy growth directly in front of the doorway.

Eagle struggled to rise, leaning on the wall of the cave. He immediately bumped his head, and discovered that he could not quite stand erect. He was amused at the thought of the lanky Old Man, even taller, living in this shelter. For there seemed little doubt now. This must be the winter lodge of the old outcast.

Why had he so carefully kept knowledge of it from the injured Eagle? The young man could only wonder. It might be simple enough. The Old Man had probably lived here for many winters. His very life depended on the fact that no one knew of his existence. Naturally, he must be cautious about revealing his secret dwelling. Such knowledge in the wrong places would become rapidly fatal. Yes, Eagle conceded, it was a reasonable way for the strange old outcast to behave. Actually, the fact that he was still alive proved its success.

Eagle hopped on his one good leg toward the entrance.

There seemed to be a lightly worn path, hardly more than a game trail, coming from the left and turning into the cave.

He thrust his head into the open sunlight and almost recoiled from the unexpected sight. Immediately beyond the thin tangle of brush which screened the cave's mouth, there was a breathtaking drop to the river below. Eagle now realized that the cave must be very near the top of the bluff and verified this impression by looking upward. It was only a short distance to the rim, so near that he felt he could almost touch the edge. Then he became dizzy at the thought and pressed himself back against the stone again.

From where he stood, Eagle could look down on the tops of the trees along the river. Only the very tallest reached their heads almost on a level with his eyes.

He looked to his left, at the path which was the only means of access to the cave. It snaked along the face of the rock, very narrow in places, overhung by brush, partially obscured by the great chunks of rock which had broken away from the mass. Eagle could understand how he had failed to see it from the camp below. It was no wonder the Old Man's lair had never been discovered.

He looked for the camp and for some time failed to find its location. Finally he identified the big sycamore by a strange shaped crotch among the upper branches. Only then did he realize what had caused his difficulty. The entire area, the gravel bar, the fire, the pool where the heron had stood, were all covered by the flooded river. At the recently abandoned campsite, the water would be deeper than a man's head.

Most impressive, however, was the manner in which the river now spread across the valley, wider than a long bowshot. In the meadow and along the slope, only the tips of the gnarled sumac protruded, now stripped of leaves. *Aiee*, thought Eagle. The Old Man had truly saved his life. Even the bloated buffalo carcasses were gone from the base of the bluff, washed away by the flood. Eagle wondered about his spotted mare.

Along the river, the trees were also partially bare, the dying leaves brushed away by the force of the wind. The bright autumn-colored foliage still clinging would soon drop also, leaving only the green of the cedars and the dead brown of the oaks. The Moon of Falling Leaves had come.

Close behind this thought came another. If the Moon of Falling Leaves had come, the moons of winter could not be far behind. Cold Maker would be back, with his deceptively dangerous series of minor attacks, through the Moon of Madness and the Long Nights Moon. Eagle now realized that he must winter here.

He was not overly concerned with this, except for his disability from the injured leg. Had not his own brother Owl wintered successfully in the mountains once, though starting with nothing but the breechclout around his loins?

Eagle looked again at the way the cave was situated. Almost perfectly, he saw. The mouth opened to the south or a trifle east of south, perhaps. That would let the morning sun warm the cavity. Even better, the spot was completely protected from the north winds by the massive bluff. Likewise, snow would be no problem, blowing over the rim and the hidden cave, to drift deeply among the trees along the river.

He could see only two problems, water and firewood. Both were plentiful below but must be carried up the narrow trail. He could not do this himself, but it would be no problem for the Old Man. Once more, he thought uneasily how dependent on the strange outcast he had become for his very life.

He looked inside the cave again, at the rawhide bundles of dried meat. Was there enough, he tried to estimate, to sustain two men through the Moon of Snows and the Moon of Hunger? If the winter was mild and open, it might be possible to hunt, but this raised yet another question.

Eagle would certainly not be able to use his leg for several moons. He would have to rely on the hunting ability of the Old Man, and he had no indication that the mysterious recluse had any hunting ability at all. Eagle had never seen him hunt.

Puzzled, Eagle tried to remember whether he had even seen the Old Man carry a weapon. He could not remember. Was there a spear or lance? No, he decided. Perhaps a walking staff, but nothing more. The Old Man had no horse with which to hunt except for the puzzling possibility that they had crossed the river on a horse. But if so, where was the animal now?

Nor could he remember seeing a bow and arrows. Was it possible that the Old Man had survived completely as a scavenger? That might partially explain the outlandish garments, the odd animal smell about the mysterious figure. It might, Eagle told himself with amusement, explain some of the Old Man's repulsive personal habits and his bad stomach.

He turned and was startled to see the Old Man approaching, only a few steps along the ledge. Once again, Eagle was both irritated and perplexed by the noiseless approach of the other.

As if in answer to Eagle's earlier line of thought, the Old Man carried a staff in one hand and in the other a crude short bow and three arrows. There was a bundle of firewood on his back, and a full waterskin dangled from his shoulder.

"You are alive," the Old Man grunted a gruff statement. "Good."

He lowered the waterskin carefully, tossed the firewood aside, and tossed the walking staff to Eagle.

"There is your stick."

It was, indeed, the very staff he had lost in the meadow. Eagle examined it while the Old Man laid aside the bow and arrows. He started to ask the circumstances of its recovery, but realized that he could not expect a direct answer. The Old Man had simply picked up the object along with the exhausted Eagle, he supposed.

He only nodded thanks and turned to help drag the firewood to a dry spot inside the cave's mouth.

Once more he puzzled over the mysterious comings and goings of the Old Man. And he now added one more question to those which remained unanswered. Why was it that when the Old Man was absent, Eagle could remember very little about him? A short while ago, he had been unsure about what sort of weapons the Old Man carried. It had been difficult, even, to remember what the man looked like.

Eagle shook his head. He must have come very close to drowning, to affect his memory so.

CHAPTER 13

Eagle adjusted poorly to confinement in the shallow cave. Always active, he fretted at the forced inactivity. It was not only the limitation of movement from his injury but from the cramped confines of the shelter. Even when he emerged from the cave door for a chance to stand upright, there was nowhere to go. His unstable, hopping gait, with one leg and his stick, was unsafe to negotiate the narrow trail. No more than a step or two was available to him before the ledge narrowed dangerously.

His entire life had been spent in the open, with room to move about. The People, with their skin lodges, were a tribe of the open prairie. In the summer the lodge covers were lifted to allow the breezes to circulate. Many people slept outside in good weather, or under the thin shelter of the brush arbors that were erected for shade. The only limitation to the freedom of vision or of movement was the far distant horizon.

Even in winter, when the band drew into closer camp, there was still the feeling of the open. The People erected their lodges nearer together and built snow barriers of brush and sticks on the north side of the camp. Some families even built a brush shelter around the north and west sides of their individual lodges. When the snow came, it could be banked deeply around the lodge for added warmth.

Still, with all the confines of winter camp, there was never the feeling of entrapment that Eagle felt now. Even in winter, a person could move a few steps outside the lodge, breathe the crisp, clean air of the open prairie, and look as far as the horizon.

By contrast, the tiny, musty cave seemed ready to close in on the frustrated Eagle. It reminded him of a time in his childhood when the Elk-dog band had camped near a village of Growers. There had been a successful hunt, and the People had a great surplus of robes and meat. It was decided to spend some time in trading, exchanging the products of the hunt for the corn and squash cultivated by the Growers. Eagle remembered that his mother, the Tall One, had welcomed the opportunity to acquire some of the foods not usually available to the People.

In the course of the association with the Growers, some of the children naturally began to play together. Eagle, always gregarious by nature, had formed a friendship with a boy about his own age. They knew little of each other's language but managed to communicate, with the hand-sign talk and with the universal language of childhood.

In due course, Eagle had gone one day to his young friend's lodge. He had been curious to see the inside of these strange lodges, set permanently in one place. The structure was half in the ground and half out, the sides built of logs and mud instead of the familiar poles and skins.

Eagle had entered, entranced, blinking in the dimness at the long strings of corn and dried vegetables hanging from the domed roof. There was a smell about the place, the animal smell of habitation. Light and ventilation were poor, and suddenly Eagle felt that the place was closing in on him. Panicky, he looked around the lodge. There was only the one exit, behind him. The mother of his friend, grinding corn in a stone mortar, looked up and smiled in a friendly way, but it was useless.

Eagle bolted from the lodge, drawing deep breaths of the open air. He had never, since that day, entered one of the Growers' lodges without a momentary return of panic.

It was with much the same feeling that he now regarded the cave. His mind told him that it was an ideal shelter against Cold Maker. Yet at the same time, he constantly fought the feeling of entrapment that the close confinement produced.

When the sensation became overpowering, Eagle would hobble to the ledge and merely stand for a time, breathing deeply the open air and gazing with longing at the far horizon.

There had been a day or two after the violent activity of the flood when he had doubts about his leg. There was more pain when he moved. He was tempted to unwrap the skins and have a look but was hesitant. The bone might be partly healed, and to remove the splints at this time would undo all his progress.

Instead, he stretched the leg before him, sighted carefully down its length, and finally determined that it was relatively straight.

He had fairly well overcome his general stiffness and the annoyance of his more minor injuries by this time. Except for the night of the flood, with his extreme exertion, his head no longer throbbed very much.

Eagle felt that he was recovering well, and perhaps this made his imprisonment even worse. He longed to make his way down the ledge to the river, to bathe and swim in the clear pool he could see far below.

Once long ago, he had seen a captive eagle. It was in the possession of the Northern band. The great bird stood on a perch before the medicine man's lodge at the Big Council, a thing of wonder to look upon for all the children of the tribe.

They had been cautioned not to alarm the bird but had been allowed to watch as the medicine man tossed it strips of meat. The eagle deftly caught the bits of food in one claw, standing on the other. It was fettered to the perch by a rawhide thong around the foot, but its keen eyes showed the untamable spirit of a wild thing.

Now Eagle remembered the captive bird and thought of

himself in the same light. Here he was fettered to the stark rock of the bluff by a useless leg. If he could only spread his wings like his namesake and fly out above the river and the trees, across the open prairie.

Startled, Eagle held his wandering thoughts in check. For a moment there, he had almost believed that it was possible for him to launch himself from the ledge and fly. This concerned him greatly. He was not accustomed to such daydreaming. He had always been a practical, logical person. Why, since his injury, was he constantly thinking strange, mysterious thoughts, his mind wandering in flights of fantasy?

Could it be that he had been injured more seriously than he had realized? The blow to the head—had there opened some flaw, some crack that would admit an evil spirit of some sort?

He sat down and examined his head carefully with his fingertips but found nothing. The bump behind his ear seemed to be healing well, without a flaw in the skin of his scalp. The dry scab was almost ready to loosen.

He wondered if it was possible for a small spirit to slip through such a slight wound before the healing began and remain inside. He wished that he might ask his brother Owl about that possibility. Eagle had never wondered much about such things, but he was certain that Owl would know.

Yet another possibility occurred to him. Could he be relating poorly to the spirits of this place? Surely the spirits of a brooding stone bluff would be different from those of the open prairie.

He thought of the affinity of the Red Rocks band of the People for their favorite area. They had formed such an attachment for the spectacular red stone bluffs and spires that they camped elsewhere only temporarily.

Of course, that was a favorable association. Could not he, Eagle, have an unfavorable relationship to the gray river bluff? He had had strange, otherworldly thoughts and night visions ever since his accident. Only a moment ago he had thought he was an eagle. There was the strange thing the night of the flood, the horse that wasn't there. Perhaps his vision was affected, too. He had mistaken the heron in the water for the Old Man.

Ah, yes, the Old Man. That was something else. Suppose, thought Eagle, that there is some evil spirit about this place. Could it, over many winters in this cave, have affected the Old Man's mind, making him behave strangely and irrationally? It was an idea worth considering.

But, no, if it had been really harmful, the Old Man would not have survived. And as for Eagle himself, no actual harm had come to him, at least not yet.

In fact, he had been quite fortunate. Several things had been very good for him. He had not been killed in the fall. He had managed to acquire the beaver sticks and the calfskin to treat his injured leg. His life had been saved, twice at least, by the Old Man.

Perhaps the spirits of the place were neither good nor bad, but only different. It was certainly like nothing Eagle had ever experienced.

He hobbled back inside the cave and settled himself restlessly to try to sleep. He wished again that he could discuss the entire matter with Owl.

CHAPTER 14

The Old Man was absent a great part of the time. He would simply appear unceremoniously and leave without warning. Occasionally Eagle would waken in the darkness from a sound sleep and feel the presence of the other man in the cave. Sometimes he could smell the strange mixture of odors that was characteristic of the old recluse. At other times, he would hear the resonant snore and realize that the Old Man had returned.

Yet there were times when Eagle could not have told how he knew. There was a strange feeling of spirit, an awareness of the other's nearness. It was not a particularly frightening thing but a trifle unnerving. It seemed to be somehow a part of the entire spirit of this hidden cave. Eagle, never one to spend time in meditation, now had it forced upon him by circumstances. There was no one to talk to in the Old Man's absence, and Eagle found himself pondering the meaning of the strange thoughts of the Spirit-World, which recurred again and again. There seemed to be something about this gray-stone bluff that encouraged such thoughts. Sometimes Eagle would question again the possibility that he was already dead. Could he, after all, have been killed in the fall, and could this be the Spirit-World?

Such thoughts usually occurred in the darkness of night. By the time the rays of Sun Boy's torch touched the cave's mouth again, Eagle was ready to scoff at such nonsense. He had also noticed that such whimsy was always completely dispersed by the presence of the Old Man. In spite of the fact that the old outcast was somehow intertwined in the mystic spirit of the cave and the cliff, his presence seemed to drive away the mysticism. It was impossible to watch the repulsive oldster, gulping, belching, scratching himself, and continue any semblance of spiritual thoughts.

Communication was very limited when the Old Man did deign to stay for a while. Most of his time was spent in sleep, much to the irritation of Eagle. It seemed sometimes to the young man that the oldster was hibernating like the bear, and he would wonder again at such a strange thought. Even during waking periods the Old Man was uncommunicative. Often the best answer one could expect to a direct question was a noncommittal grunt.

It must be said that the Old Man never climbed the rocky trail to the cave without bringing an armful of wood for the fire and perhaps a skin of drinking water. Even this became a source of irritation for the crippled Eagle. He was totally dependent on the Old Man for wood and water. The other had a tendency to wait until the waterskin was empty and the last stick on the fire before bringing more.

Eagle would hoard the last few twigs, the last precious swallows of water, as long as possible. True, there had been no time when the fire had died completely, and he had never become really thirsty. Still, the unconcerned attitude of the Old Man was a matter for some worry. What if, tomorrow or the day after, he did not return for a longer period than usual? There was no way in which Eagle could traverse the path to the bottom of the bluff to procure fuel and water. And it bothered him to be dependent for life on the whimsy of a crazy old man.

Suppose the Old Man was delayed in his return or misjudged the amount of wood or water required? A single night without the fire could result now in death from exposure. The annual advance of Cold Maker from the far mountains of the north was readily apparent. It was the Moon of Long Nights, when Sun Boy's torch seemed ready to go out.

Three times already, a powder of light snow had drifted across the prairie. Eagle knew that his position was a tenuous one at best, and it was extremely frustrating to be able to do nothing about it. If only he could walk a little. Desperately, he attempted to practice, with his stick and his good leg, but was limited to the few steps along the ledge. He could not even stand erect enough to practice inside the little cave.

Eagle developed a daily routine. A look outside, perhaps the few steps on the path, then a meager meal from the carefully hoarded supplies. If the day proved warm enough, he would sit outside and study the broad expanse of prairie, longing to be far off toward the distant earth's rim somewhere. Then, as the all too short day saw the lengthening shadows of Sun Boy's torch, Eagle would again chew some of the dried meat.

He was beginning to doubt that there was enough to last until the Moon of Awakening, when things would be better again.

Most annoying about the food supply was the Old Man's attitude. On the occasions when the Old Man was present, his major occupations were eating and sleeping. At any time he was awake, the gaunt old recluse seemed to be shoving food into the bottomless expanse of his large mouth. Eagle grimaced to see the other demolish a bundle of dried meat at one sitting that would have lasted the younger man several days.

Finally it became apparent that the food supply could not possibly last.

"Uncle," Eagle began, "there will not be enough food for the winter."

The Old Man nodded, unconcerned, and reached for another strip of the dried buffalo meat. He began to chew and slurp noisily.

"We will get more."

But he initiated no action, no plan or suggestion. Eagle

throttled the impulse to shout at the Old Man, to attempt to force on him the importance of planning ahead. It would be of no use. The Old Man would do as he wished anyway.

Much as Eagle longed for human companionship, he sometimes wished the Old Man would not stay when he stopped by the cave. His presence was an irritation, and his inroads on the diminishing food supply were becoming a greater threat with each visit. Then, after such thoughts, feelings of guilt nagged at Eagle. His very survival depended on the chance that the Old Man might continue to favor him with visits, bringing fuel and water.

The first heavy snow began in the darkness one night. Eagle had seen the signs before night began. The wind was changing, the small animals scurrying frantically to shelter. There were few birds, most having followed Sun Boy on his annual circle to the south.

Eagle carefully evaluated his small pile of wood, perhaps enough for three sleeps. He was concerned that if Cold Maker dumped large drifts of snow, the trail to the cave would be impassable when the Old Man returned with more fuel.

Uneasily, he prepared for sleep as darkness fell. If he used just enough fire to break the chill of the cave and wrapped warmly in the various furs and skins to keep from losing the heat of his body, he would require less fuel.

Eagle awoke, aware of a strange difference in the light of the cave. Sleepily, he blinked at the drifted snow, banked half across the shelter's opening. Thin, watery sunlight washed across the lap of the drift and reflected on the cave's roof.

Awake now, he rose with alarm and hobbled to the opening. The white drift was waist-deep, packed in the space between the cave's mouth and the fringe of brush. Eagle stretched to see the trail along the bluff. He found that it was not only impassable, but that, with the heavy drifting snow, in some places he was unable even to identify where the path had been. It must melt before the Old Man could return.

Panic seized him for a moment, and he stepped backward, nearly falling over his frozen waterskin. Eagle picked up the object and returned to the fire. He must think carefully now. *Aiee*, Cold Maker had dealt him a treacherous blow.

He would eat snow to satisfy his thirst, he resolved, saving the precious water. His fuel supply was meager, and he must keep the fire barely alive. Food was already carefully hoarded.

Eagle turned to the rack to lift a new rawhide packet of meat. He had eaten the last scraps from the previous one last evening.

To his surprise, the bundle was light, much lighter than he expected. Anxiously, he turned it over, then pulled the skin wrapping apart.

On the back side, where the bundle had rested against the cave's wall, was a gaping hole in the rawhide. Some small creature had discovered the treasure of hoarded food. The strips of dried meat had been systematically removed one by one and carried away through some hidden crevice. Even the few scraps that remained were fouled with the creature's droppings.

Eagle's food supply was now only half what he had thought. A moment of panic gripped him, and he frantically fumbled for the one remaining pack of food.

Its weight reassured him, and Eagle carefully opened the bundle to evaluate the contents. The blackened strips of dried meat were intact. Quickly, his mind began to perform more logically, racing ahead to plan for the utmost use of the painfully scant supplies.

He could fast, he believed, for several days at a time. It was common, when a young warrior reached manhood, to spend days alone, fasting and in communion with the Spirit-World. This led to visions, by which a person might identify his medicine animal, his spiritual adviser. Eagle well remembered his own vision fast and his discovery of his spirit-guide.

Why could he not fast again, for three or four suns at a

time, perhaps? Then he could eat and fast again. He would become very weak, but in this way he could remain alive until, perhaps, his leg was healed enough to make escape from the ledge a possibility.

That, of course, would depend on the melting of the snow. *Aiee,* there were many things to consider.

Eagle ate enough snow to slake his thirst and carefully rewrapped the food bundle. Almost reverently he set it aside on the very top of the willow rack, the contents untouched. Now would be as good a time as any to begin his plan of fasting to conserve his meager supplies.

CHAPTER 15

Eagle soon found that the drifted snow in front of the cave was not entirely undesirable. Sun Boy's torch reflected through the upper part of the opening and warmed the interior much more effectively than before. In addition, the partial closure of the opening prevented the back eddy of wind from swirling into the cave so fiercely. The fire required much less fuel to maintain a semblance of warmth. It was much like partially drawing the door skins on one's lodge, Eagle realized.

By far the most impressive thing about the next few days, however, was the dreaming. Fasting was known to produce visions. That was the whole purpose of the vision quest of the young warrior. Yet for Eagle, this strange place and the odd spiritual quality of thought that he had noticed before seemed more intense than any he had ever experienced.

He had a vague feeling of regret that he had not spent his vision quest in this place. How much more meaningful it might have been. Eagle had been a trifle disappointed in his vision quest. Nothing much had happened. He had fasted for three sleeps and had achieved the bright, clear-headed thinking that goes with one's fast. But his vision would not come.

He knew that the coming of one's vision should be the most important thing in life. This was the time when one's medicine animal would reveal itself. He had dreamed of many animals, but there was nothing special.

Eagle knew that many of his friends and acquaintances felt deep emotional and sacred ties to their spirit-guides. Of course, no one must ever tell anyone of his medicine animal or his vision quest, so he was unable to discuss it or compare experiences.

After four sleeps, he had wakened to find an eagle hovering near his camp. The bird looked long and fixedly at his eyes, then suddenly screamed its piercing cry and swept away on fixed wings in the wind. Eagle had been impressed by the free spirit of his namesake and decided that this was his medicine animal, his spirit-guide.

Ever since, however, he had wondered. His brother Owl had obviously more powerful ties to his medicine animal. Eagle had wondered what that animal was. Not an owl, surely. The medicine man had a good-natured tolerance and amused liking for kookooskoos, the strange soft bird of the night. Yet he lacked the reverence one holds for his spirit-guide.

Possibly Owl's medicine animal was a buffalo. His medicine was that of the herds. The young man had proved his skill with buffalo in a contest to expose Two Dogs, the false prophet.

Thinking such thoughts, vague regrets that he had somehow missed the closeness with his spirit-guide that others felt, Eagle drifted off to sleep and dreams.

His dreams were many, varied, and sharply real, but were not of medicine and spirit-guides. Most were of his childhood.

The dream state carried him back to his first memories of Sweet Grass, now his wife. They were very young children again, learning together in the Rabbit Society. Eagle could see that Long Elk, their teacher, had great respect for the young wisdom of the prettiest girl in the group. The instructor, who was also Eagle's uncle, would sometimes tease the youngster.

"Sweet Grass will be a good wife for someone," Long Elk would remark to no one in particular.

Young Eagle would blush and become self-conscious.

There came the day when Eagle was stalking a rabbit in the woods. Ahead in a clearing he saw movement. Carefully, he moved forward, ever so slowly, in the best stalk of his young life. Finally the young hunter parted the last leafy screen and discovered the girl, Sweet Grass, playing with one of the other girls.

They had made a number of toy lodges from leaves of the cottonwood, rolling each leathery leaf into a cone. The pointed toys were arranged in a circle, just as the lodges of the Elk-dog band were.

Eagle watched and listened to their chatter. Then quietly he crept to the fringe of cottonwoods near the stream. Here and there, where the People had cut saplings for lodge poles, lush second growth sprang from the stumps. The boy selected the largest, glossiest leaf he could find and quickly pinched off the stem. With his thumbnail, he split the tip, tore horizontal slits near the point, and folded miniature smoke flaps. Then he rolled the leaf into a cone and pinned the edges with a thorn.

Just as Eagle returned to the clearing, a stray breeze caught the girls' tiny encampment, scattering leaf lodges across the ground. Sweet Grass and her friend scurried to retrieve them, while Eagle stepped forward to help.

In a short time, the little make-believe camp was restored, with much giggling and laughter. Then Eagle brought out the lodge he had made, to set it proudly with the others. It was much larger, since the special leaf he had selected had been as broad as a man's hand.

"This is our lodge," he boasted to Sweet Grass, "yours and mine. It will have more than thirty skins and will be the biggest in the tribe!"

The girls giggled behind their hands, but Eagle saw what he wished. Behind the embarrassment on the pretty face of Sweet Grass was another look, one of admiration and confidence. She saw this childish boast not as mere empty words, but as a statement of fact. She became serious for a moment.

"I will manage your lodge well," she smiled.

From that day forward, neither of the children seemed to have any doubt. When the time came to marry, Eagle and

Sweet Grass would be together in their own lodge. It was a fact that was accepted by the entire band.

In others of his dreams, Eagle saw the friends of his childhood grow to maturity and marry. He and Sweet Grass came together in the Moon of Roses. Their lodge was not made from thirty buffalo skins, but it was only their first. A larger lodge could come later. The joyous occasion was marred only by the absence of Eagle's brother. Owl, at that time, was missing for several years and was believed dead.

The most impressive of Eagle's dreams in the cave, however, continued to be of stories around the evening fires. Nearly every time he fell asleep, he became a child again, sitting before a flickering fire, with his knees hugged tight against his chest. And many of the most impressive stories dealt with the Old Man of the Shadows.

Eagle's grandfather, the Coyote, was always a favorite storyteller, and he loved to tell stories of the Trickster. The children had heard the tale of the bobcat's tail many times but never tired of it. They always listened intently when the Trickster, disguised as a hollow tree, furnished a place for the spotted cat to hide from a hunter. The Trickster had, however, been planning revenge on the bobcat for some now-forgotten insult. In his hollow-tree shape, he left a knothole, which allowed the cat's long tail to protrude and blow in the breeze. The hunter seized the tail and cut it off close to the tree's trunk, and the tail of the spotted bobcat has been short ever since. At this point the children rolled on the ground with laughter.

More frightening were the tales where the Old Man of the Shadows would unexpectedly turn into a gigantic bear or other fearsome creature. At these times the children huddled together and cast anxious glances at the darkness behind them.

Eagle dreamed of these times and would awaken frightened and trembling, still a child in the cave's darkness.

Somewhere between these two Man of the Shadows stories were those which were merely amusing. The ingenuity of the Trickster was legendary. Harassed by enemies or natural phenomena, he could change himself into a bird and fly out of the difficulty. Again, when hungry, he would change to some creature of different eating habits to satisfy his needs.

Coyote had once told of a time when food was scarce, and the Trickster became a heron, hunting in the pools of the stream for small fish and frogs. The People did not eat such things, but they were natural diet for the heron. Reliving this story in his dreams, Eagle suddenly awoke, understanding blossoming in his brain. Had he not actually seen the Old Man change to a heron and fly away?

Within a few heartbeats, however, he was wide awake, irritated at himself for his confused thoughts. How could he continue to confuse the repulsive old recluse with the Trickster of myth and legend? Perhaps he, Eagle, was going mad.

Still irritated, he rose to replenish the fire, carefully hoarding the few remaining sticks. With some degree of concern, he noticed that the wind had shifted. The howl and whistle around the crevices of the bluff's face had a different sound, and Eagle sensed that Cold Maker was coming again.

Anxiously, he evaluated his fuel supply, and the remaining strips of dried meat. His plight would soon become desperate. Even if he burned the sticks that formed the willow rack at the back of the cave, he had no more than two suns' fuel.

Once more, his survival would depend on the return of the crazy old man. If, Eagle reminded himself grimly, the trail to the cave was not impassable with drifted snow already there or that to come soon.

CHAPTER 16

Cold Maker blustered and howled, and Eagle wrapped himself in every scrap of fur available in the cave. He fed the tiny fire only enough to keep it alive, carefully saving every splinter of the willow rack for fuel.

Sun Boy was not seen at all through that day, only the dull gray of the sky. Through the narrow opening of the cave's mouth, Eagle could see occasional flurries of powdery snow.

One more time, he counted the sticks of dried meat. It was obvious that his food, used with care, would last several days longer than his fire. He had been so concerned about food, and now it was a cruel twist that he would likely freeze before his meat was gone.

Eagle stuck his head and shoulders out of the cave mouth above the drift, to see if any chance growth could be used for fuel. He could find nothing within reach. Halfway down the path along the bluff's face was a scrawny growth of dogwood, but the trail was drifted and impassable. The sparse thicket directly in front of the doorway was deeply buried in the snow. Maybe he could dig down to it. The activity might at least warm him.

He was soon forced to abandon that effort. His hands were becoming stiff with cold and his body chilled by the cutting bite of the wind. He looked up at the sky as he slid back into the cave.

There above him, stretching enticingly, Eagle saw the branches of a dead tree. He had noticed it before, a tree growing on the rim of the bluff. Almost within reach, the dry twigs rattled in the wind, taunting the freezing man. Eagle wished for only a handful of twigs from the vast supply above him. A few sticks might make the difference between life and death. He reached as high as he could but lacked an arm's length. He limped back inside and brought his walking staff. He had tried to burn it, but the wood had been too green to catch fire.

Clumsily, Eagle swung the stick, attempting to knock loose a few dry twigs. He could barely reach the overhanging tips, and the tiny sticks and shreds of bark that were knocked loose were carried away by the wind.

Desperate now, he attempted to throw his staff at the lower branches. He realized that he risked losing it but felt that he had to try. It was growing dark, and his tiny fire would hardly last the night.

His throw was good, and the staff rattled against the dead limbs, but none fell. The walking stick itself, even, hung a moment before dropping back into the drifted snow. It was out of reach, but it mattered little. Beaten, Eagle crept back inside.

He searched the crevices of the cave's corners for any chance twigs carried in by pack rats but found only a few. He attempted to burn a rawhide pack that had contained food, but it burned poorly. The greasy smoke and smell were not worth the small amount of heat generated. Carefully, he fed tiny twigs from the pack rat's crevice, keeping the fire alive.

Eagle wondered whether he would survive until the coming of Sun Boy. If the storm subsided and the sky cleared, there was a chance that he could last a little longer. The heat of Sun Boy's torch would warm the cave in the daylight hours.

Unfortunately, the storm showed no sign of abating. As darkness fell, Cold Maker howled even louder. Eagle shuddered, wrapped the ragged skins around his body, and huddled over his little fire.

It was almost full dark when Cold Maker's assault rose to a climax. The rock itself seemed to shudder with the force of the gusting wind. At the height of the storm's fury there was a heavy cracking sound, like that when the real-fire strikes nearby. Eagle wondered dully at this. There was no real-fire in winter, in Cold Maker's storms. It occurred in summer, in the Moon of Thunder.

The crack was followed by a heavy grinding sound, and for a moment Eagle thought the rock of the bluff itself was falling. Surely, there was a tremble in the very stone. Before he had time to move, even, a different sound was apparent at the cave's mouth. It was a crackling and snapping, like a large animal moving through dead brush.

Against the dimness of the almost dark sky, Eagle saw the shape of interwoven limbs and twigs descending, crashing downward across the cave's entrance. Only then, as the crackling ceased, did Eagle realize what had happened. Cold Maker's massive assault had toppled the dead giant at the top of the cliff. It took only another instant for him to realize that this might be his salvation.

Quickly, Eagle began to pick up broken twigs from the floor of the cave. As the fire grew, lighting the interior, he could see more easily. The tree had pivoted downward, the large upper limbs coming to rest on the ledge as the smaller branches broke away. There, available almost within arm's reach, was enough fuel to last for days.

Eagle laughed aloud in triumph and shook a fist in the teeth of Cold Maker's howl. He piled more sticks on the fire, and the cave began to warm. The young man spread his robe and basked in delicious warmth. He removed his moccasins and rubbed the blood back into his numbed feet. The stinging burn of his skin told him that his escape from Cold Maker had been very narrow. His feet had nearly frozen.

He allowed himself the luxury of a stick of his carefully hoarded dried meat and followed it with several handfuls of snow. Then, with a full belly, warm and comfortable, he stretched out to sleep.

At first, sleep would not come. Eagle was too elated over his victorious escape from Cold Maker. Finally his senses calmed, and he drifted toward rest. As he neared sleep, one of his last thoughts was to note that the wind was subsiding. Having been defeated, Cold Maker had now given up the battle. Eagle smiled to himself in triumph.

He dreamed again, and the visions were again of his childhood. The warmth he felt was that of the fire in his father's lodge. He saw the dream image of his mother, the Tall One, sitting beside him and cradling his small brother, Owl, to her breast.

Eagle had, from the time he was small, understood that his mother felt something quite special about her boys. He was long in coming to an understanding. It was somehow related to the fur on his father's face. Heads Off was the only man among the People with fur on his face, but Tall One obviously considered this a desirable difference.

Then there was the puzzle of his father's name. Why, small Eagle had wondered, was he called Heads Off? For many men of the People, their names seemed appropriate. Many Robes, the Real-chief, was recognized for his wealth and his skill in its acquisition. Small Ears, chief of the Eastern band, was aptly named. There was an old woman called Bear's Rump. In her youth, she had bravely attacked a bear from behind with a spear, to save her husband's life. Even the name of his grandfather was appropriate. Coyote, clever and inconspicuous, but with a chortling little laugh that sounded much like the summer call of the small prairie cousins of the wolf.

But "Heads Off"? There seemed no reasonable explanation for such a designation for his father. Had he, young Eagle wondered, chopped the heads from defeated enemies at some time in the past? The boy hardly thought so. It seemed out of place as an action of his father's.

At last Eagle had summoned courage to speak to his grandfather.

"Uncle, why is my father called 'Heads Off'?"

Coyote chuckled.

"It was a joke, small one."

He settled more comfortably against his willow backrest and told the story. Hunters of the People had found the young man, injured and unconscious, with his horse grazing nearby.

"We had never seen an elk-dog before or a man of your father's tribe. He wore a hard shiny headdress and strange garments. We thought he might be a god."

Coyote chuckled at his own past naiveté.

"Then the god woke up and reached to take off his crested headdress. We had thought it was his head, crested like that of the green lizard. So, it appeared to us that he was taking his head off. And, little one, that is how your father got his name."

He smiled and patted young Eagle's head.

"Of course, I did not expect him to become my daughter's husband. That was much later."

Big Footed Woman brought meat to the two at that point, interrupting the conversation. Eagle chewed at the warm slab of hump ribs and watched his grandfather do likewise. Coyote was a noisy eater, thoroughly enjoying his food. He loudly munched and slurped, pausing to belch loudly on occasion.

Then the dream began to fade. Something was wrong. Coyote ate noisily but not that repulsively. Eagle struggled up from his sleep state and tried to put the sounds in their proper place.

He was in the cave again. The fire flickered cheerily, and there was the feel and smell of another presence.

There, across the fire, sat the Old Man. It was he, making the eating noises. With wide-eyed alarm, Eagle watched the repulsive old recluse calmly stuff the last scrap of carefully hoarded meat into his cavernous mouth. He chewed noisily, gave a great gulping swallow, and licked a few crumbs from his fingers.

"Uncle!" Eagle almost screamed at him. "That is the last of the meat!"

The old man nodded noncommittally, belched loudly, and scratched his belly.

"Yes, we will have to get more!"

He passed wind loudly, apparently oblivious to the smell, and rolled in his robe to sleep.

Eagle did not know whether to laugh, cry, or scream out in angry rage. At the moment, he thought that he had never felt such complete frustration with another person.

CHAPTER 17

After he had calmed somewhat, Eagle began to wonder how the Old Man had managed to reach the cave. He limped over to the entrance to look out. The storm had passed, and Sun Boy was rising to a cloudless sky. The entire world was dazzling white, painful to the eyes.

A quick look down the cliff trail showed not much more actual depth of snow. Cold Maker's assault had been mostly bluster. Eagle could also see where the Old Man's tracks had broken the smooth surface of the drifts along the path. In a place or two, the tracks wallowed through, or rather across, the deeply drifted trail. It still appeared extremely dangerous. Once again, Eagle was forced to admire the abilities of the Old Man. And again, he realized that only by skill and agility, as well as resourcefulness, could the other have survived at all. He, Eagle, would have hesitated to attempt the drifted trail even without his injury.

He spent some time breaking up and carrying into the cave as much firewood as he was able. At first he hesitated to break sticks and interrupt the Old Man's sleep. Then his bitter resentment overcame his natural thoughtfulness. The Old Man deserved no better. Almost with pleasure, Eagle began to break the largest sticks he was able. To his disappointment, the noisy cracking seemed not to bother the sleeper in the least. In fact, the breaking of sticks was partially muffled by the vibrating bull bellow of the Old Man's snores.

Sun Boy was past his highest position in the south when the sleeper awoke, stretched and yawned, belched, and scratched his crotch. He poked around the cave a little and then spoke.

"You have no more food?"

Eagle was furious, but controlled his temper. The Old Man was his only source of supplies.

"No. Rats ate part of it."

The other nodded, as if this were no great problem.

"I will look for some."

He picked up his outlandish fur cape and quickly slithered over the drifted snow at the cave's entrance. It was not an easy task. The heavy branches partially blocked the way, but the agile oldster wriggled through. The Old Man paused a moment, picked up Eagle's lost walking stick, tossed it to him, and moved on. Eagle could watch him make his way cautiously down the trail.

Once before he reached the frozen river, he was again obliged to wriggle on his belly across a drifted place.

Eagle watched the Old Man slip quietly over the ice and into the woods. There was probably a herd of deer wintering somewhere upstream. Fresh meat would certainly be welcome. He waited expectantly for the Old Man's return, but all was quiet along the river.

By the time Sun Boy neared earth's rim again, Eagle had realized that the Old Man would not return this day. Once more, his spirits slipped into the depths of despair. What if the other, for some unforeseen reason, did not return at all? Again, he hobbled to the cave's mouth and wondered if he dared try to descend the path. It would be necessary to try in a few sleeps if the Old Man did not return.

Eagle's neck hair bristled suddenly as a shuddering scream broke the quiet of the frozen prairie. He identified the sound immediately. There was no other sound in the world of the People like the hunting cry of the great cougar, the real-cat. It resembled nothing so much as the scream of a woman in terror or distress. The Old Man was not the only one seeking meat this night.

As dusk deepened, the call of the great hunting cat was

repeated at intervals. Eagle, though uneasy, was not unduly alarmed. The thought crossed his mind that this cat might on occasion use as a den the cave where he was now a prisoner. Still, the fire would surely keep the animal away. At least Eagle devoutly hoped so. He built the fire a little higher.

Sun Boy had retired to his lodge before Eagle saw the real-cat. The animal could be seen clearly against the snow on the opposite hill by the silvery light of the rising moon. Fascinated, Eagle watched the creature's fluid motion as it threaded among the bare stalks of the sumac thicket. Once it stopped and looked up at the bluff. Even at the great distance, Eagle had an eerie feeling that the yellow eyes of the cat were looking directly into his. *Through* his eyes, even, into his very soul. He wriggled backward into the cave and crouched a little lower but was too fascinated to cease watching.

The cat came to a slight rise and paused to lift the spine-chilling hunting cry again. Finally it disappeared into the trees along the river. Eagle breathed more easily. Again he told himself that the real-cat was no actual threat to him. It was simply that now, in what he thought to be the Moon of Hunger, the great cats were traveling widely, hunting for deer herds in the dense timber along the streams. This had appeared to be a large male, probably hunting to feed cubs in some remote den.

From time to time Eagle heard the chilling screams again, as the cougar moved in its hunt. He was uneasy, unable to rest. Several times he rose to watch the moonlight on the snow-robed prairie.

It was during one of these times that he saw the deer. There were perhaps ten or more, bounding and leaping in alarm from the clawing terror behind. The herd came from the timber upriver, the area where he had heard the last hunting cry. The usually graceful animals were careless, crashing through the sumac thickets. They snorted in fear, blundering, oblivious to their path. This herd had, Eagle knew, looked recently into the yellow eyes of death. Somewhere in the woods the cougar had found meat, and one of the deer lay staining the snow with its lifeblood. It was the way of things. He hoped that the Old Man's hunt would prove as successful as the real-cat's.

Eagle quickly rejected an intrusive thought that flitted across his consciousness. Could it be that the one hunter had become the prey of the other? Such things had happened. The Old Man had been stalking the same band of deer as the cat. Could he have become the hunted? Eagle tried to thrust the idea from his mind, but was only partially successful.

Still fascinated by the hunt scene which he imagined had occurred in the woods, Eagle continued to watch. It was some time before he saw motion on the ice of the river upstream. It was a slow, deliberate thing, some large dark form moving out of the shelter of the trees and onto the open ice. In a few moments, Eagle identified the real-cat, partially carrying and dragging a limp form. He craned his neck to see, almost dreading what he might discover.

The cougar dropped its prey to rest for a moment, and Eagle sighed with relief. The still body was that of a deer, not the lanky frame of the Old Man.

Now the beast's movements were merely interesting to watch. How clever, Eagle thought, to use the smooth ice of the stream to drag the heavy body of the night's prey. It would be much easier than carrying or dragging over rough ground. He wondered where the den might be. Somewhere downstream, he supposed. It was known that the great cats hunted over a limited territory, but that territory might be as broad as a day's journey for a man. How far, he wondered, could the cougar carry its kill?

He saw that the course of the animal was crossing the frozen river toward the base of the bluff below him and wondered at this strange thing. Could it be that the real-cats' den was in another cave in this same area? And, if so, why had he not heard their hunting cries before?

Eagle was still pondering this when another startling realization struck him. The direction taken by the cat would bring it across the river directly at the foot of the path to the cave. Now, thought Eagle, it is time to be alarmed. There was no other place for the cat to go. This narrow trail led only to the hidden cave. Frantically, Eagle attempted to understand the meaning of this strange thing. Surely the real-cat would not make a mistake. It would know where its own lodge was located. Perhaps this cougar and its mate had not yet had their cubs, and were searching for a den.

Yes, that must be it. They may even have used this cave as a den before. He thought of the musty animal smell he had noticed when he first awoke in the cave. How long ago it seemed now.

Now the real-cat was dragging the deer carcass off the ice and starting up the path. It was time for action. Eagle quickly threw an armful of wood on the fire, and the cave began to be uncomfortably hot from the leaping flames. Now what about a weapon? He glanced around the cave, realizing he had nothing except his knife, little help in combat with a real-cat.

His eyes fell on his walking staff, and he picked it up. No, too short. The cougar could strike with a longer reach than that. A longer stick? Eagle hastily hobbled to the entrance, and with a mighty effort broke loose a branch from the dead tree. Almost at the same time, an idea struck him. All animals except man fear fire. He could use his long branch as a burning torch to fend off the attempts of the cat to enter. He thrust the small end of the branch into the flames and sprang to see the cougar's location.

To his dismay, the great cat was nearly halfway up the trail and making good progress. It paused a moment, looked him full in the face with its strange yellow eyes, and kept coming.

Would the branch never kindle? Eagle fanned it with his hands, knowing as he did so that it was useless effort.

He took another quick look, and the cat was still climbing,

dragging the deer carcass along the ledge. By its actions, Eagle now realized that the animal considered this cave its own and was prepared to fight for territory.

His torch sputtered into cheery flame, and he left it in place in the fire to allow it to become well started. Now he could hear the approach of the cougar, the sound of its breathing, the swish of the deer carcass across the snow. He picked up the blazing brand and waited inside the entrance.

Eagle had not long to wait. The head and shoulders of the gigantic cat appeared in the opening, and the lips parted in challenge. As plainly as words could have, the snarl conveyed the message.

"You are in my lodge!"

Eagle's lasting impression was one of sharp white teeth. Though frightened, he remained in control of his senses, almost calm.

"My brother, I am sorry, but I cannot let you have this lodge. My life depends on it!"

He thrust the burning end of his long branch directly into the snarling face. The cat turned its head away to avoid the blow, but the brand seared across the left jawbone, down the neck, and slid beneath the animal's left foreleg.

With a scream of rage and pain, the cat flung itself backward. For a moment, Eagle thought it would go over the edge, but it twisted quickly and recovered. Then, with long, leaping bounds, the great cat sprang down the path, across the ice, and out of sight in the woods, still running frantically.

Eagle, dripping with sweat that was not entirely from the overheated cave, sat down weakly to rest.

CHAPTER 18

As Eagle ventured to look from the cave after the retreating cat, he saw a dark form stretched against the snow. For the space of a heartbeat he felt panic, the flash of a thought that there were two of the animals. Would he now have to confront the cougar's mate? He gripped his still smoldering brand.

Quickly, however, he realized that the furry body in the snow was not alive. It was not the form of a real-cat, but of its prey, dropped by the cat as it started to enter the cave. Eagle slid partially out onto the snow for a better look.

In the bright glow of the full moon, he could see the fat yearling buck, hornless now for the season. Immediately, Eagle realized that the encounter with the real-cat had been greatly to his own advantage. He wriggled forward across the snow bank until he could reach an outstretched leg.

Eagle was weakened by his recent exertion, as well as cold, hunger, and lack of physical exercise. The effort was great, but he managed to move the still-warm body of the deer a little way. Once moving, it required less effort. The slippery surface of the snow made the task easier, too. Soon the young man slid, exhausted, to the floor of the cave, his prize beside him.

Eagle laughed aloud and would have danced a dance of victory on his one good leg, except that the roof of the cave was too low. *Aiee,* now he had food and fuel, and in quantities to last until the time of greening. It would not matter if the Old Man never returned at all. Even his injured leg would be healed by the time his food was gone. He laughed again, took a little dancing hop, and bumped his head. This sobered him somewhat, and he turned to the task at hand.

He decided to butcher out the deer, but to leave the dressed carcass at the cave entrance. Cold Maker was useful for some things, and the keeping of fresh meat was one of them. Eagle could merely carve off the required amount for his daily needs from time to time. But it would be necessary to remove the entrails to prevent the meat from spoiling.

He slit the belly, and pawed out the loops of bowel, tossing the offal outside on the snow. Later, when he had more strength, he would throw the refuse over the edge of the bluff.

When he came to the liver, he handled it as a valuable prize. Carefully, he removed the dark green pouch of gall from the under surface and laid it aside. Only then did he slice a bite from the raw liver's edge to pop into his mouth. For many generations, the People had recognized the powerful medicine of liver. It was especially useful in the late winter and spring, helping to rejuvenate those who had lived for the winter on dried meat. There was no way to preserve the liver or its useful medicine. It must be used immediately, unless it could be frozen, and then only for a short while.

Eagle ate more bites of liver as he worked, his appetite ravenous for the healing, rejuvenating properties in its juices. Then, he hollowed a space in the snow bank, and placed the remainder in the hole. Perhaps it would keep for a short while.

He cooked strips of meat from the flank, and methodically gorged himself with fresh food until he became uncomfortably full. Finally, his fire carefully banked, Eagle rolled in his robe to sink into a deep, dreamless sleep.

He was awakened sometime later by a resonating roar. He started to leap up in alarm, his knife already in hand, before he became aware of his surroundings.

It was full day outside, Sun Boy already climbing. The fire burned low, and on the other side of the cave lay the sleeping figure of the Old Man. Another hollow snore vibrated the cave, and Eagle realized what had just awakened him.

He was irritated. Everything had been moving so well when he went to sleep. He had been able to see the means of his survival, and this did not necessarily include the help of the Old Man. He still struggled with mixed feelings. Without the Old Man's help, Eagle would never have survived at all. Yet he had come to resent the presence of the other, his gluttony, his disgusting personal habits, even his appearance.

He sat dejected, staring at the sleeper. The next rattling snore boomed through the cavernous nose. Whimsically, Eagle recalled a game he had played as a child. The children had discovered that an empty rawhide pack carrier was an amusing thing to play with. By placing one's mouth near the opening, one could enhance the sound of the voice. The hollow vibrations of the rawhide could enable even a small child to imitate the sound of a bellowing bull, the boom of the small green heron, or the deep voice of the giant frogs in the rushes.

The odd thought occurred to Eagle that the snore through the Old Man's huge nose acted in much the same way as the vibrating of a shout into the emptiness of a rawhide pack. Interested by this idea, he leaned forward to study the next bellow.

Only then did he see the burns. Along the left side of the Old Man's face and neck were the marks of a fresh encounter with fire. Nothing else could cause such an injury. Even the fur on the chest of his outlandish garment was scorched.

Once more the flood of doubt assailed the young man. How did it happen that such strange ideas intruded into his mind? Still, the thought refused to be quieted. How had the Old Man suffered such similar injuries to those Eagle had inflicted on the real-cat? Again, he thought of the incident of the heron, that of the horse in the river, of the smell-cat routing the Head Splitters. If Eagle could grant himself the one small belief, that of the actual existence of the Old Man of the Shadows, all the mysteries would be solved. Even the falling of the tree to supply fuel for survival might be related.

Eagle shook his head, confused. As a child, he had been

completely convinced of the reality of the stories of the Trickster. Only with the practicality of the adult had he put aside
the cherished beliefs of childhood.

Yet in the presence of the Old Man or under the influence of
his medicine, Eagle kept returning to so many childhood
thoughts. Only a moment ago, he had almost been ready to
tell himself that the Old Man had changed to a hunting cougar to bring him food. He must rid his mind of such ridiculous
things. Surely there was a reasonable explanation for the Old
Man's burned face. Eagle concentrated on a wart on the end
of the sleeper's nose. There could be no question of its reality,
and he found it comforting to think of things about the Old
Man that were definitely *not* supernatural.

Under Eagle's steady scrutiny, the sleeper became restless,
stirred in his robes, and finally awoke. For a long moment he
looked steadily into Eagle's face and then sat up.

"Ah, you have meat! Good. I have seen none!"

The two men built up the fire, and the Old Man sliced
chunks of the venison from the haunch in the snow. Eagle noticed that the other did not even seem curious as to how the
meat had been acquired. Well, the ways of the oldster were
strange. One thing he must ask, however.

"Uncle, your face is burned."

The Old Man actually jumped with surprise, and his hand
flew to his cheek as if to see if it were really true.

"Oh, yes," he mused, as if trying to remember, "I slipped
and fell into my own campfire. I have become clumsy in my
old age."

Yes, and crafty too, thought Eagle. The explanation given
by the Old Man was certainly easy and logical. Possibly true,
even. But somehow it was not easy to believe that a wiry individual who could scale the bluff like a mountain goat would
be clumsy enough to fall into his own campfire.

CHAPTER 19

During the next few days, the Old Man stayed in the cave. He seemed weak and tired, and without energy to accomplish much except to eat and sleep. Eagle was alternately irritated and sympathetic toward the old recluse. He shared the liver he had buried in the snow bank and then resented the repulsive way the other gulped and slurped the precious substance.

In due time, the burns healed, and the Old Man regained a quickness in his glance. Soon he began to take short explorations down the bluff, sliding on his belly over the drifted snow where necessary.

Eagle was grateful for the time of the other's absence. There was something about the very presence of the Old Man that made it difficult to think rationally. Eagle felt that, all things considered, it might be better to be alone than under the overwhelming influence of the Old Man's spirit.

So it was that, when the Old Man finally departed, Eagle was relieved. He had regained his confidence, and it could now be seen that Cold Maker had done his worst for the season. The young man could begin to look forward to a return to his people. True, it would be many sleeps yet before he could travel, but he felt that the worst was now behind him.

The Old Man said no good-byes, simply made his way down the bluff as he had so many times before and did not return. It was the next day before Eagle began to relax, having convinced himself that the other had actually gone.

As the days passed, the drifts of snow on the path dwindled, and Eagle began to plan his departure. It must be timed properly. He must give his healing leg all the time he could, yet leave the cave before his food was entirely gone. Water was also a consideration. He had done adequately on snow water, but the supply was dwindling. He longed to plunge his face into the cool clear water far below and drink until he could hold no more.

By far the most important consideration, however, was the injured leg. Eagle counted on his fingers the moons that had now passed since the ill-fated hunt. The Moon of Falling Leaves had given way to the Moon of Madness and the Long Nights Moon, then the Moon of Snows. It must now be nearly past the Moon of Hunger. The time for healing of the broken leg should soon be sufficient.

Carefully, Eagle unwrapped the rawhide and the splints to examine the leg. It was pale, thin, and wasted, and very dirty. Dead skin flaked from the surface as he rubbed and scratched. The leg was not entirely straight but adequately so, Eagle thought. Gingerly he felt the swollen lump of new bone which had formed at the broken area.

Next, he attempted to put weight on the leg and nearly fell. His muscles, long disused, simply refused to obey when he called on them. After several tries, he managed a limping hobble. *Aiee*, it would take much practice!

It was the Moon of Awakening before Eagle felt ready to try the path down the bluff. He had been partway several times, but today he intended to go all the way to the river. The People were traditionally great swimmers and bathers, and the inability to cleanse himself of his body smells was becoming a source of irritation to the young man. That, with the warming days and increasing odor of his own excrement, had become a major source of annoyance to him.

He stood for a time in front of the cave, savoring the earthy scent of the warming south wind.

A long wedge of geese clamored overhead, moving north for the season. Eagle flew with them in spirit. He always felt the

call to move to new places, new campfires, in the Moon of
Awakening. The instinct was stronger this year, made more urgent by enforced inactivity. He watched the last of the long
line of geese and picked up his walking staff to attempt the
path.

Small sprigs of green poked tentatively from damp crevices
on the south face of the rock. Buds on the cottonwoods below
him swelled to a golden yellow, promising greening soon. It
was altogether a day of good medicine for being alive, and for
attempting the descent to the river.

The first few paces were easy, and then the path dropped
abruptly, a broken and irregular surface. Every small pebble
or crevice imparted a side motion to his weakened leg. By a
third of the way down, his calf muscles began to ache and
throb, and he sat on a boulder to rest. Momentarily, he considered returning to the cave to try another time. Then, as he
rested, he decided that this was to be the day. Even if he must
spend the night at the bottom and climb back the following
morning, he must make this move today.

At the narrow part of the trail halfway down, the overhang
of the bluff made balance difficult. Eagle was forced to use his
weak leg more than he wished. Sweat beaded his face, and he
was glad to stop again for rest when the trail widened. He wet
his lips from a snow-melt trickle in the rocks, and partially
filled his waterskin. A little farther, and he could feel the
freshening moisture from the river's surface. Leaning on his
staff to ease the ache, he rounded the last boulder and limped
onto the narrow strip of land sloping from the bluff to the
water. New grass sprouted from the soil, and the current of
the river lapped invitingly against the shore.

Eagerly, Eagle hobbled forward and stretched flat on his
stomach to drink. He gulped great mouthfuls of the clear,
fresh water until he could hold no more. He rolled to his back
and lay resting in the sun for a time. Then he filled his waterskin and laid it aside.

Shedding his shirt and leggings, he waded cautiously into the chill of the water. Though his teeth were chattering, he joyously splashed and cavorted, briskly moving to keep warm, scrubbing at his chest, arms, and body. He plunged completely under the surface, blowing and spouting as he surfaced. Then he loosened his long hair and rubbed it between his palms to remove the winter's smoke and grime.

When the water's chill began to cause the muscles of his injured leg to cramp, Eagle waded ashore and sat in the sun again, straightening and rebraiding his hair as it dried.

Already, he was planning his departure. Tomorrow, he would pack the meat that he had smoke-dried and prepare to return to the People. He would have to travel slowly, but that should be no problem. He would return to the winter camp of the Elk-dog band. They should not have departed yet.

Eagle smiled to himself, thinking of Sweet Grass and the children. It would be good to see them. They might think him dead by now.

He pulled the shirt over his head and was just tying his leggings when he happened to glance up at some slight motion across the river. There on the opposite shore sat a well-armed party of horsemen. They seemed amused and appeared to have been watching him for some time.

They were Head Splitters.

Eagle's first impulse was to run, but there was nowhere to run. The narrow strip of land on which he sat was only a few paces long and even fewer in width. The only way off the strip was into the water or back up the path to the cave. A few lunges of the enemies' horses would bring them across the river and onto the bar. Eagle could be started up the path by that time, but in no way could he move rapidly enough to escape the agile warriors behind him.

Quickly, he made a decision. He would approach the situation boldly and with confidence. The enemy warriors were amused already. If he could keep them relaxed and interested, they would not kill him immediately. Then eventually there might come an opportunity to escape.

Yes, his best path was to behave in a confident, unafraid manner and see what might occur.

Eagle smiled and waved cheerfully to the horsemen across the river, and then nonchalantly turned his undivided attention to the tying of his legging strings. Let the enemy make the first move.

CHAPTER 20

Great concentration was required to look down at the legging strings and not at the enemies. Eagle could all but feel the eyes of the warriors watching his every move. He half expected to feel an arrow's searching thrust in his vitals but need not have worried. The Head Splitters hooted and howled with laughter at his bold maneuver. When he could delay no longer, Eagle straightened and faced the horsemen. A large man who appeared to be their leader kneed his horse forward into the edge of the water.

"*Ah-koh*," he called to initiate the conversation. Except for the initial greeting, the exchange was carried on in the universal hand-sign talk of the plains. Eagle knew hardly a word of the other's spoken language, but there would be no problem in understanding.

"How are you called? What is your tribe?" the enemy chief signed.

"Mine are the People, called by you the Elk-dog People," Eagle answered.

It could do no harm to reveal that. The Head Splitters probably knew it already or could soon tell from his garments and the style of his hair.

"How are you called?" the chief persisted.

Eagle had decided to reveal as little as possible and to rely heavily on his injury to make him appear nearly helpless. He shrugged and spread his upturned palms wide.

"I am called many things by some people." (Laughter from the opposite shore.) "Today I am the Broken-legged One."

More laughter followed as Eagle lifted his legging to show the injured member. The entire idea of a helpless enemy showing his injuries to those about to capture him seemed uproariously funny to the Head Splitters. He decided to push his luck to the limit.

"Don't go away," Eagle signed. "I will show you!"

Very gingerly, he limped to the water's edge and plunged boldly into the river. The Head Splitters roared with laughter. Good, thought Eagle. A man does not laugh and kill at the same time.

There was a little time to think as he swam slowly toward the enemy horsemen. Eagle thought he recognized their chief. It was not uncommon for individuals of enemy tribes to know each other by name, especially their leaders.

Once or twice a year, bands of the People, moving to another campsite, would encounter a band of Head Splitters, similarly engaged. Neither group would wish to initiate combat on the open prairie, with the attending risk to the women and children. So, three or four warriors would accompany a chief from each tribe to a neutral point between the two moving bands. The chiefs talked in sign talk of the weather, the hunt, and prospects for the winter. Often they would tell the enemy where they intended to camp. They could be easily located anyway, and the appearance of trust and goodwill was important to keep the enemy off guard. Sometimes the opposing chiefs, through repeated contact over the years, developed a healthy respect, almost a friendship, for each other.

Eagle had participated in these informal meetings many times and now thought he recognized Bull's Tail, one of the most respected of the enemy chiefs. He was known to be a strong leader, firm but fair, and unfortunately merciless in combat.

It had, in fact, been Bull's Tail who had captured Eagle's brother Owl while the young medicine man was on his vision quest. Owl's subsequent travels and eventual escape had been an important part of his rise to position as one of the tribe's most powerful medicine men.

Now, this same Bull's Tail was the leader of the party into whose hands Eagle had fallen.

Eagle's knee struck the river's gravelly bottom, and he stood to wade ashore. He limped heavily, partly feigning his disability, and stopped at a grassy spot on the bank. There he sank to a sitting position and lifted his ragged legging to show the emaciated leg.

The enemy warriors closed around him, and one poked experimentally at the weakened leg with his spear butt.

"Stop!" Eagle shouted and signed indignantly. "You will injure this leg!"

Laughter followed, but Bull's Tail rode forward, dismounted, and spoke harshly to the warrior. Then he turned again to Eagle.

"How are you here?"

Eagle shrugged again and pointed to the rocky cliff.

"My horse carried me over the bluff."

"No!" Bull's Tail refused to believe. "Your leg is nearly healed. You could not live the winter here alone. Someone has helped you."

The chief turned and spoke to a couple of young warriors, who turned their horses and moved along the stream, apparently searching for Eagle's companions. Eagle wondered for a moment where the Old Man might be, but soon abandoned that pathway of thought. He had more than enough problems of his own.

"I do not believe you," Bull's Tail was signing. "We will find your people."

Eagle assumed an innocent air and shrugged again.

"You have found the Elk-dog People before."

He had gone nearly too far. It was a thin reference to the fact that in the past few clashes, the Head Splitters had been soundly defeated by the People. An angry mutter ran through the group.

"No, my chief! It is only that such farseeing scouts as yours must surely find any of my people who are here!"

Bull's Tail stood, studying his prisoner, not convinced. He seemed puzzled.

"Wait!" he signed suddenly. "I know you! You are the son of Hair Face, the Elk-dog chief!"

Aiee, thought Eagle. That is too bad. If he thinks I am an important prisoner, he may hold me for ransom. Still, that very fact might insure good treatment. He smiled innocently.

"As you say, my chief. But now, I really must go. My people will be looking for me."

He rose and limped painfully a step or two before he was stopped by a warrior with a spear. The man is careless, thought Eagle. I could easily take his spear from him and kill him with it. But it could serve no useful purpose. He would remember this man as a weak spot when the time came for escape. For now, he turned to Bull's Tail in apparent bewilderment and pleased surprise.

"You wish me to be your guest?"

In the general laughter, even Bull's Tail seemed amused.

"Yes, Broken Leg. You will stay with us for a time."

CHAPTER 21

Eagle lay wakeful, near the center of the Head Splitters' night camp. The sleeping figures of Bull's Tail's warriors were scattered under the trees in postures of rest.

His hands were not tied. Eagle had managed to avoid that by appearing cheerful and cooperative, and by exaggerating his limp all he could. The Head Splitters had thoroughly searched the timber for some distance up and down the stream, without success. They failed to notice the path to the cave. Actually, Eagle himself could not see the path from where they sat, and no one seemed inclined to swim a horse across the river just to look at the other side.

There were obviously a minimum of hiding places anyway, along the stark face of the rock.

Eagle had made such a point of his inability to walk that Bull's Tail directed one of the young men to take the prisoner up behind him on his horse. Initially, the warrior was sullen and resentful, but Eagle was so profuse in his thanks, so cheerful and appreciative, that the man relaxed.

There was no doubt in Eagle's mind as to the seriousness of the situation. At any time, if he angered some of the party or even if it became inconvenient to leave him alive, he would be killed without hesitation.

Still, it seemed wise to appear as if he did not consider his life in jeopardy. Eagle chattered happily to his captors, saying nothing they could understand, but adding enough sign talk to keep them interested. The Head Splitters viewed all this with tolerant amusement, paying little actual attention to the prisoner. After all, he was under the protection of the chief. Bull's Tail would probably demand many horses and robes for the release of the prisoner to his people.

Meanwhile, Eagle carefully observed the party from the back of the horse. There were fourteen men, all well armed. In this small a number, they were probably a hunting party, but if opportunity offered, they would instantly become a raiding or war party.

He evaluated each man singly. There was Bull's Tail, leader of the group, capable and careful. There was the man who had threatened with the spear, a man not too intelligent but dangerous because of his loyalty to his chief.

Most of the rest of the party had nothing remarkably important. They were young, somewhat careless, and should be not too difficult to deal with when the moment came.

There was one man whom Eagle studied with great care. He was somewhat older than the rest, very quiet and not taking part in conversation and laughter. He was heavyset and ugly, with a scar across one cheek distorting his mouth into a perpetual smile. The smile had no humor, though, and from his dark glance and the well-used look of his weapons, Eagle realized that this was the most dangerous warrior in the party. He would be the first to reckon with when the escape attempt came.

Now, after a half day's travel, the party had camped for the night. A scout had been posted, and as he settled himself for sleep, Eagle caught the eye of Scar Face. There was no doubt about the meaning of the man's stare, as he readied his weapons beside him and wrapped up in his robe. There would be no possibility of slipping away with this experienced warrior on guard.

Eagle wrapped a ragged scrap of robe around his shoulders and moved closer to the fire. Bull's Tail had tossed the prisoner the robe as they prepared to camp for the night. Nights could be quite cold in the Moon of Awakening. It was not so much from kindness or compassion, Eagle realized, but from practicality. The prisoner would be of little value for ransom if he were dead.

He turned restlessly and glanced once more, for perhaps the hundredth time, at the Seven Hunters in their nightly journey around the Real-star. Their position told him that it was still a long while until the rising of Sun Boy. A hunting owl hooted somewhere, and a distant coyote called to his mate. Scar Face was snoring, but Eagle knew that the seasoned warrior could be alert in a moment if the situation demanded.

It was not long after those thoughts fluttered lazily through Eagle's mind that the opportunity came to test this observation. The quiet of the night was shattered by a yell of terror from the edge of the camp. Sleeping forms came rapidly awake, fumbling for weapons.

In the space of a few heartbeats, the running figure of the sentry could be seen. The young warrior was stumbling, dropping his robe and his weapons as he lurched toward the sleeping area. As he retreated, the man kept looking over his shoulder at the darkness behind. There was no question about it. Here was a man running in terror of his life.

Questions were shouted back and forth, but apparently there were no valid answers. Eagle was completely bewildered. What could possibly cause a capable, well-armed warrior on sentry watch to become suddenly a babbling terrified child?

Someone had thrown some dry fuel on the fire, and it now flared into life, pushing the shadows back among the trees and into the night. Eagle glanced at the scar-faced man, who was methodically fitting an arrow to his bowstring as he peered into the darkness behind the terror-stricken sentry.

There were gasps and exclamations of wonder as a huge dark form tottered out of the night in pursuit of the retreating man. For a fleeting, brief moment, Eagle felt that this hulking figure must be the embodiment of all the evil spirits of the earth. The creature raised its head, and the darkness was shaken by a vibrating roar. Eagle's neck hair prickled, and there was a sensation of fear that made his skin crawl.

Then he realized, as the creature came closer, that it was completely understandable. As many terrors of the time of darkness fade before the light, so did this one. By the light of the campfire, now growing brighter, the creature became more visible as it approached. It could now be identified as a gigantic bear, walking erect on its hind legs. The great jaws opened again in a roar of challenge.

Very quickly, Eagle determined the things about the rapidly changing scene. First, this was no ordinary bear. It was not the usually seen black bear, the digger of roots and grubs. This was the real-bear, the bear with white-tipped fur and evil disposition, the bear-that-walks-like-a-man. And, to all appearances, this particular bear was the grandfather of all real-bears.

The other idea that formed in Eagle's mind as he watched the rapidly developing scene was one of hope. This incident might provide an ideal opportunity to escape.

He rose and clutched the robe around him, ready to run at the proper moment.

CHAPTER 22

Among the tribes of the plains, there were some who hunted and killed bears for food and fur. Others avoided them.

For the People, the bear held a special place. Because of the occasional habit of the bear, especially the real-bear, of walking erect, the People had from earliest times considered it a sort of semihuman creature. Therefore, it was wrong among the People to kill the bear unless absolutely necessary. To eat the meat of the bear was forbidden. That would be, in the custom of the People, the equivalent of cannibalism.

Among the Head Splitters, there was no such taboo. They were known to seek and actively hunt the black bear and to relish the meat of the animal. There were people in Eagle's band who had, as prisoners of the Head Splitters, witnessed feasts in which roasted bear's flesh was devoured by all.

Now, as Eagle tried to decide the proper moment to run, a strange thought occurred to him. It seemed to him that this real-bear was here to help him. With the age-old attitude of respect accorded its kind by the People, it seemed logical to Eagle that this, the grandfather of bears, would look kindly upon him. Equally possible was the fact that this bear was bent on wreaking vengeance on the Head Splitters for centuries of persecution of its kind.

Eagle had little time to ponder the philosophy of the situation. The great bear was rapidly approaching. Most of the warriors were scattering in confusion, but Scar Face calmly faced the monster. He dropped to one knee and pulled his bow to full draw. The string twanged, and the arrow leaped forward, striking the bear in the fleshy part of the shoulder, where it joined the thick neck. There the shaft remained, sticking out front and back.

The real-bear roared again, this time with rage and pain. It dropped to all fours and charged directly at Scar Face, who was attempting to fit another arrow. He was bowled over by the rush, and the sweep of a giant claw ripped across his chest and belly. The mortally wounded warrior's scream was muffled as the bear lifted and shook him in its mouth as a dog would a small striped ground squirrel.

There were shouts, and an ill-aimed arrow or two flew harmlessly past the raging animal. Eagle did not see. He was running, plunging into the thickest part of the brush and timber along the stream. If only his leg did not weaken. He attempted to favor it, limping as he ran. He wished for a moment that he had a better idea how much the leg would bear. Could he be overprotecting it? There was no way to tell, as he continued to run, bumping into trees and rocks in the darkness.

Exhausted, he paused to rest against the bole of a great sycamore. It was beginning to grow light, the sky in the east graying with the false dawn. Eagle's breath, steadying now, no longer came in ragged gasps. He could begin to hear, above his own breathing, some sounds of the morning. Birds called, the chuckling ripple of the stream sounded through the trees, and a distant crow greeted the dawn with hoarse cawing.

The smooth harmony of these blending sounds was interrupted by the sharp snap of a stick behind him. Eagle whirled. There was time only to catch a glimpse of a warrior, in the act of swinging a heavy stone club. Eagle started to dodge, and the reflex probably saved his life. Instead of a solid blow to the victim's skull, the club glanced from the sycamore, striking with slanted force above his ear. Eagle felt himself falling, saw lights bursting in his head, but was unconscious before he struck the ground.

He was still lying on the ground when he awoke, but in completely new surroundings. It was daylight, and he was lying in a very small opening, ringed by thick dogwood bushes. Eagle cautiously moved his head to look around and became aware of a throbbing headache. There was a lump over his ear which seemed as big as one of his wife's cooking stones. He groaned.

Then, for the first time, he noticed that he had a companion. The Old Man was lying nearby, looking directly at him. He made the hand sign for silence, then added wordlessly, "They are looking for us."

Eagle nodded, sending new waves of pain through his skull.

"You are not dead. That is good," signed the Old Man. "We will stay here till dark. Then we must go."

He sank back, and for the first time, Eagle saw that the other was wounded. There was a great smear of blood from an injury to the right side of the neck, where the muscles of the shoulder joined it. Now that Eagle looked more closely, it was apparent that the Old Man was very weak from loss of blood.

"How did we come here?" Eagle signed. "How were you hurt?"

Weakly, the Old Man signed a terse reply.

"I brought you here after you were hit."

He turned his head away, and Eagle knew that the conversation was at an end. Further attempts at questioning would be useless. Eagle sank back, staring at the leafy canopy overhead and wondered at the events of the past day.

He had no idea where he was now, but there had not been time to travel far. They must be no more than half a day from the cave. Strange, he thought, that the Old Man should turn up again. How had he happened to be close by when the Head Splitter struck the escaping Eagle? Had the Old Man been hiding near the Head Splitter camp when the real-bear came? And how had he been wounded?

Eagle raised his head to look again at the wound, risking considerable discomfort to do so. There was nothing really unusual about the ragged slit in the wrinkled skin of the Old Man's neck. It was much like every other arrow wound Eagle had ever seen.

Only then, as he lay back, did Eagle think again of the dramatic scene by the Head Splitters' night fire. He saw again in his mind's eye the scar-faced man fit the arrow and loose it at the charging real-bear. Now, in his memory, the arrow struck, wounding the great animal and turning its rage on the tormentor.

Once again, the strange feelings of things beyond understanding came over Eagle. There was much here beyond the usual. How, for instance, did it happen that the Old Man's wound was virtually the same as that suffered by the real-bear?

What had happened to the Head Splitter who had struck Eagle down? Had he been killed by the Old Man? By the bear? Or, in the time of darkness, were the two the same?

Eagle knew that he might never find out. The close-lipped Old Man would never answer such questions.

CHAPTER 23

Sun Boy was drawing near his lodge in the west when the Old Man awakened. Eagle had slept little. Most of the day he had wrestled with his confused thoughts about the old recluse. There had been times in the past few moons, usually in the dark of night, when Eagle believed that he had the answer. Surely, this was the legendary Old Man of the Shadows. The young man could list countless little incidents that seemed to prove the theory. Some major incidents, too, not the least of which was the encounter with the real-bear.

Eagle saw that the Old Man had opened his eyes and was gazing at his companion, unmoving, waiting. Eagle realized that the Old Man might have been awake for some time. A curious thought occurred to him. At no time during the long afternoon had there been the slightest suggestion of a snore. Apparently the Old Man could snore or not, at will.

Eagle started to sit up, and the Old Man again cautioned silence.

"The Head Splitters are still near," he signed. "We will move soon."

"Where is the real-bear?" Eagle signed. "Will it return?"

There was almost a smile on the wrinkled old face. Surely, a twinkle in the Old Man's eyes. It was a new expression, one Eagle had not seen before. The oldster seemed to be actually enjoying the game of hunter and hunted.

"*Aiee*," he signed, "I hope not!"

Ruefully, he rubbed his injured shoulder.

"Where are the Head Splitters?" Eagle tried again.

The Old Man shrugged indifferently.

Shadows lengthened, and a night bird called somewhere. From the direction Eagle supposed the stream to be located, the high trilling call of the small spring frogs made a constant sound.

"We go now?"

The Old Man shook his head.

"No. Not yet."

To Eagle it seemed a long time, and he was becoming chilled in the gathering darkness, before the Old Man cautiously rose.

"Come!"

He led the way into a hidden pathway among the thickets of dogwood, willow, and hackberry. The growth became thicker, the night blacker, along the river. Eagle had no idea of direction.

The Old Man stopped suddenly, and Eagle collided with him in the darkness.

"Now be especially quiet," the Old Man whispered. "Here, hold this."

He placed Eagle's hand on the thong around his waist, and moved slowly forward. They were approaching the river. Eagle could hear the rippling of the stream across a shallow riffle. His guide paused only a moment and stepped into the water. The icy chill rose around Eagle's ankles, and in a moment the two were wading downstream, across a gravelly bottom.

The Old Man paused and pointed in the dim starlight. There around a tiny campfire on the shore, Eagle could discern the squatting figures of several warriors. The fringe of trees was narrow at this point, and he could see the pale darkness of the open prairie beyond. Silhouetted against the starry night sky stood the enemies' sentry, watching.

Eagle began to realize the Old Man's plan. They apparently must pass the Head Splitters' night camp. On the open prairie, they might be seen, even in the starlight. In the river, with the sound of their movements muffled by the song of the water, they might pass unnoticed.

They were almost past the point where they were nearest the enemy camp when Eagle's foot betrayed him. The injured leg had begun to numb from immersion in the icy stream, and he did not feel his footing well. A fist-sized stone rolled from under his step, and he fell heavily into the shallow water.

Instantly, there were shouts from the camp, and men came running. Someone was attempting to light a torch for better visibility. Eagle scrambled to his feet, despairing of anything but recapture. The armed warriors were practically upon them.

Suddenly the yells of the approaching Head Splitters were drowned in another sound, the roar of an angry real-bear. The sound came from so close beside him that Eagle nearly bolted directly toward the enemy. Before he could react, the Old Man spoke, directly in his ear.

"Come on," he hissed, "make noise!"

Another roar split the night. The enemy warriors recoiled. They had no desire to pursue a wounded real-bear into the darkness. There was a flurry of excited conversation. One man loosed an arrow, which whispered harmlessly past the fugitives. The Old Man roared again, and excited yells admonished the bowmen not to anger the real-bear.

Now the Old Man was splashing deliberately downstream, making no attempt to hide the noise of their passage. There was no pursuit. The excited voices behind them faded in the distance as they continued to run.

Out of sight and hearing from the Head Splitters' night camp, the fugitives waded ashore and paused, exhausted. Eagle's breath came in ragged gasps, from the unaccustomed exercise, and painful spasms chewed at his injured leg. The buzzing in his ears was like that of bees at swarming time, and his vision was misted.

The Old Man leaned tiredly against a tree, eyes closed, breathing heavily. His left hand clutched at his injured shoulder, where the arrow wound had opened and begun to bleed again. His right arm hung limply.

By the time the two had recovered their breath, a reddish glow in the east signaled the rising of the half-moon. Eagle touched the Old Man's arm and pointed. Wearily, the Old Man opened his eyes and stared dully at the red-orange glow.

"*Aiee!*" he muttered without emotion. "We must move!"

He took a long deep breath and seemed to gain stature and confidence. He beckoned.

"This way!"

Eagle was hard put to keep up with the long stride of the Old Man. Their course led across open prairie, but followed the lower contours of the rolling hills. Once, when it became necessary to cross a ridge, the Old Man paused a long while to study their back trail. Finally, he grunted in satisfaction and moved swiftly across the open flatness of the hilltop.

It had become considerably lighter in the radiance of even the half-moon. Visibility would be adequate to see two human figures for a long distance in the open grassland.

A band of antelope sprang up before them, snorting in alarm. The Old Man swung aside to follow the general course taken by the animals for a time. He was, Eagle knew, attempting to confuse the trail, mixing the tracks of the fugitives with those of the antelope. There would be expert trackers among the enemy party, and any way to cause confusion and delay pursuit would be helpful.

Shortly after the rising of Sun Boy, the deception of the roar in the night would be discovered. The Head Splitters would find the trail where the two had left the river and read the entire story. One fugitive who limped, one tall man who walked well. With some fresh bleeding from the Old Man's wound, the pursuing trackers might even discover that the companion of "Broken Leg" was injured.

Their situation was still dangerous. The enemy could range widely on horseback, in pursuit of fugitives on foot. Perhaps they should have tried to steal horses, thought Eagle. But it was too late now.

Eagle limped along, trying to keep up with the rapidly traveling Old Man. It was unfortunate, he told himself, that there were no buffalo on the prairie. To move cautiously through a grazing herd would effectively blot out their trail under the shuffling hooves.

But there were no buffalo. The great herds were still far to the south, not to return until the lush new growth returned after the time of burning. Eagle's thoughts turned to the ceremonial firing of last year's grass in the Moon of Greening. The medicine men would announce the proper time, and the new growth in its turn would bring about the return of the buffalo.

A chilling thought occurred to him. What if the enemy realized how exposed the fugitives were in the open grassland? What if the Head Splitters set fire to the prairie?

Eagle's leg was paining greatly now, and he felt that he could go no farther.

"Uncle!" he called softly. "I must rest my leg!"

The Old Man nodded understandingly and dropped to a sitting position as suddenly as if he were shot. He briefly checked the location of the Seven Hunters and the Real-star, then lay flat on his back to rest.

"Uncle," Eagle ventured after catching his breath, "where are we going?"

He had become somewhat disoriented and had seen no familiar landmarks.

"The cave!"

Eagle still did not know where that might be. In fact, he was not certain whether the water they had waded in the escape was the same as that by the bluff. It could be another loop or ford or an entirely separate stream, separated from the other by one of the ranges of hills.

As if in answer to his question, the Old Man gestured vaguely.

"There."

Eagle could see nothing in the direction indicated except rolling hills. He was still concerned about the possibility of fire.

"Uncle," he persisted, "how far? What if the Head Splitters fire the grass?"

"*Aiee!*" muttered the Old Man.

He rose swiftly and swept a quick glance around the earth's distant rim. Then he tossed a few wisps of dry grass into the air to test the slight, shifting breeze. He chuckled, pleased.

"*Aiee*," he muttered again. "What if *we* fire the grass?"

CHAPTER 24

They stopped for a prolonged rest before dawn. Eagle did not believe he could have gone farther. His leg had been throbbing, painful, becoming worse and more swollen as they traveled. When they finally lay down to rest, the cramping began. Frantically, Eagle attempted to rub the spasms from protesting muscles. He thought he would never be able to rest, but sleep came swiftly.

Then, it seemed only a moment later, the Old Man was shaking him gently. It was still in the chill quiet of the false dawn, that short time before the torch of Sun Boy catches fire.

"Come!"

The two resumed travel, and again Eagle wondered how far to their goal. It must be fairly close, he thought, because he had traveled only a half day as a prisoner of the Head Splitters. Allowing for the difference in traveling speed on foot and the somewhat circuitous route taken by the Old Man, they still must be less than a half day from the cave.

They moved on, stopping briefly to drink at a spring among the rocks.

"Stay here," muttered the Old Man.

He took a few steps among the boulders along the twisting game trail and was gone.

Eagle was glad for a time to rest, to rub the protesting muscles of his weak leg, and to let the sun warm his chilled body. He lay on his back and watched a soaring eagle climb a long spiral toward the sky, and then slant in the direction from which they had come. He wondered idly what thoughts an eagle might have. From that height, the bird could see for half a day's distance. It could even, he realized, observe the Head Splitters' camp and their pursuit. How useful that would be. Of course, if one were an eagle, there would be no need to observe pursuers on the ground. One could simply fly away.

Eagle shook his head, a little bewildered at the course his mind was taking. These flights of fancy were not the usual thoughts of Eagle, the practical warrior. His spirit had grown much in the past few moons.

The Old Man returned, as quietly as he had left. Eagle did not actually see him return, except for the last few steps. It was simply that a few heartbeats before, the Old Man was nowhere in sight. Now he was striding among the jumbled stone of the rimrock, almost near enough to touch.

"Come. They have found our trail."

There was no explanation as to how the Old Man could have learned this. It was merely stated as fact. Eagle rose to his feet, thinking for a moment of the farseeing abilities of the bird that was his namesake. He glanced at the sky, but saw no soaring eagle. Once more, he had the strange, mystical spirit-feeling about the Old Man and that there was some connection with the eagle.

And again, close on the heels of that thought, came the other, that of ridicule. Eagle could not be in the company of the Old Man for any time at all without feeling the utter impossibility of his imaginings. This was merely a strange and slightly crazy old outcast, although a very clever one. The Old Man had survived many seasons alone on the prairie, largely because of his quick wit and his ability to take advantage of any situation. To think that there was anything of the Spirit-World about the Old Man was completely unreasonable. Eagle shot another quick glance at the sky, expecting to see the soaring bird, but he did not.

Beside him, the stomach of the Old Man rumbled loudly, and an ample belch resonated from the cavernous mouth. Eagle was reminded that it was long since they had eaten.

"We will eat later," the Old Man said over his shoulder as he started away.

Eagle struggled to keep up. The Old Man was climbing to the top of the ridge. When they finally reached the level hilltop, both were puffing from the exertion.

"*Aiee!* Now we rest!"

The Old Man threw himself flat on a shelf of stone.

Eagle was irritated. To have called forth this much hurry and effort to reach a high place, only to sit down and rest, seemed ridiculous. It was only as he more fully evaluated their surroundings that he realized the reason. They were now on a high vantage point from which to see their back trail. The area over which they had just come lay spread before them, stretching into the far distance. As it would look to the eagle, the young man pondered.

In the far distance, a tiny speck moved. Across the saddle of a distant hill moved a file of horsemen, slowly, deliberately. Many times Eagle had taken part in hunting parties or war parties just such as this. There was very little about the sight that was unusual. The only different thing about this party was their quarry. The hunted were Eagle and his companion. He watched, fascinated.

The man in the lead must be the tracker. The others would follow him, single file, to avoid disturbing the trail. Second in line would be the leader of the party. Even at this great distance, Eagle thought he could distinguish the bulky form of Bull's Tail. They were moving at a fast walk.

"Uncle!" Eagle was surprised to find the Old Man apparently asleep.

"Uncle! They come!"

Without moving or even opening his eyes, the Old Man answered.

"I know. They found our trail quickly. They are good trackers."

"What will we do now?"

Eagle was surprised again at how willing he had become to depend on the Old Man for decisions. At the same time his willingness to do so irritated him.

The Old Man heaved a sigh, and slowly raised himself to a sitting position. He studied the distant hill, and finally spoke.

"We wait a little longer."

Frustrated, Eagle watched the riders as they painstakingly studied the trail. They were sweeping in a long arc, following the wandering track established by the Old Man. The pursuers were moving in an easterly direction. Now they were almost due north of the watching fugitives, and as they completed a distant turn, were nearly exactly downwind. The Old Man had maneuvered the Head Splitters into a vulnerable position.

"Now!" he muttered.

From somewhere in his shapeless garments, he had produced fire sticks. In a short while, his rubbing had produced a tiny blaze. The Old Man thrust the pinch of flaming tinder into a clump of dry grass, and the blaze leaped upward. Fanned by the south breeze, the fire spread quickly, racing down the slope in the thick dead grass.

Eagle was unable to see the enemy when they discovered their plight. The smoke was too thick, the flames moving too rapidly, spreading to right and left across the plain. Somewhere beyond the heavy gray billows he could imagine the enemy warriors wheeling their horses, attempting to find a way of escape. At very best, they would have to stop and attempt to kindle a backfire. For the present, the pursuit was over.

The Old Man was laughing, delighted. The fire had done its work well. Only a few small flames licked among the rocks of the ledge where they stood. Its spread upwind would be contained by the nearest small stream. The Old Man beckoned, and the two turned down the hillside toward the distant river bluff.

Both were exhausted, cold, and hungry. Eagle's injured leg now bothered him increasingly. At one of their frequent rest stops he took care to look at the Old Man's wound. To his surprise, the ugly injury seemed almost healed. Still, the Old Man seemed tired. He had been through much in the past two suns.

The two supported and helped each other across the river and dragged aching bodies along the narrow path. By the time Sun Boy had extinguished his torch and gone to his lodge, the fugitives had reached the cave.

CHAPTER 25

Eagle slept, the deep undisturbed sleep of exhaustion, until well past daylight. When he finally woke, it was to find every muscle in his body stiff and painful. The past two suns had required extended effort. In his weakened condition, with poor food and no exercise for several moons, any effort called forth the use of unfamiliar muscles.

He sat up, and a cramp in the back of his right thigh seized him. Hastily, Eagle grasped the painful leg and massaged deeply until the spasm subsided. Finally he was able to remain in a sitting position and look around the cave.

There, beside him on the floor, lay a piece of dried meat. After a moment, he remembered. He and the Old Man had reached the cave, ravenously hungry. The Old Man had started to build a fire, while Eagle took meat from one of the bundles. He handed one strip to the Old Man, stretched on his bed, and—he could remember no more. He must have drifted off to sleep, too tired even to eat the food in his hand. He had dropped the meat beside his bed and remembered no more until now.

The fire burned low, although the Old Man had apparently tended it since daybreak. Now, he had already departed. Once more, Eagle marveled at the resilience of the Old Man. There were few men of any age, he reflected, who could have done the things accomplished by this strange old recluse.

He fed small twigs to keep his fire alive and chewed on a stick of meat while he looked around for a waterskin. A full skin lay near the entrance, apparently brought by the Old

Man. Eagle was pleased. He could, of course, go down the path to the river, but it was comforting not to be required to.

Gratefully, he drank long and deep, once more thinking of the Old Man with mixed feelings. Once more he owed his well-being, yes, his life even, to the repulsive old outcast. Each time Eagle had been completely helpless and in need, somehow the Old Man had been able to correct the situation.

Eagle was not ungrateful. He could not be ungrateful to one who had repeatedly saved his life. It simply rankled, like a festering sore, that the means of his deliverance had come from so unlikely a source. The Old Man must indeed have strong medicine to accomplish what he was continually able to do. And, Eagle admitted uncomfortably, it raised doubts about his own medicine.

He had never wondered much about it. He had been able to accomplish the things of life necessary for his own happiness and the comfort of his family. There had been no reason to rely heavily on one's medicine. Now, in recent moons, he had repeatedly had to rely not on his own skills, or even the strength of his medicine, but on help from someone else. Perhaps, Eagle thought, he was somehow not allowing his medicine spirit to help him fully.

Eagle shook his head, puzzled. He had done it again, pondering spiritual things he had never wondered before. It must be that the spirit of this place, the gray stone of this bluff, encouraged such thoughts.

He stepped out on the ledge to watch an eagle spiraling in the sky, so distant it was no larger than a speck. Again, as on the previous day, he felt curiosity about all the things on earth that an eagle might see. There was also the strange sense of kinship with the bird that was his namesake. Perhaps he was only now achieving the oneness with his spirit-guide that he should have. Eagle heaved a long sigh. He would talk with his brother, the medicine man, about such things when he returned to the People. Or perhaps to their grandfather. Coyote was very wise.

Thoughts of his people brought thoughts of his wife and children. How he longed to see them, to hold Sweet Grass in his arms, cradling each other for warmth against the chill of the night. He hoped that she had not taken another husband yet. Of course, if Eagle returned, she and the children would return to his lodge. Still, he hoped that would not be necessary. Surely she would wait, to be sure, even though her husband was believed dead.

It was these disconcerting thoughts that finally convinced him. He must move on. If his injured leg could withstand the battering it had sustained in the past two suns, it must be ready for travel.

Eagle spent the rest of the day preparing for the journey. He had little to carry, only his meager supply of dried meat. His major preparations consisted of long periods of time spent in observing the sky, the behavior of birds and insects, and the quality of sounds as they floated across the still prairie. He must be certain of the weather before he left the cave's shelter.

Once Eagle thought he heard a horse call in the distance. Instantly, he was alert, watching intensely, wishing for the far-seeing vision of the bird high above. He could see no sign of any activity, and the sound was not repeated. Eagle decided that he had been mistaken.

His main problem as he began the journey home would be to avoid the Head Splitters. He had decided to do so by traveling at night. Darkness works to the good of the hunted. He could guide his travel by the Real-star, and rest in hiding during the daylight.

As the day drew to a close, Eagle prepared to depart the cave for the last time. The Old Man had not returned. Still under the influence of the overwhelming spirit of the place, he lingered over his dying fire. On an impulse, he took a small fragment from his precious food supply and placed it carefully on the fire as an honor to the spirits. He watched as the fire consumed the offering and then rose to depart. He wished to finish the descent along the narrow ledge before it became fully dark.

He shouldered his makeshift pack and picked up his walking staff. It might be very useful, especially since he had no other weapons except his short knife. He had puzzled long about that knife. The Head Splitters had disarmed him, of course, but after his escape, there was a flint knife of good quality in the sheath at his waist. He had finally decided that it had belonged to the enemy warrior who had struck him down. Whatever the fate of that Head Splitter, the Old Man must have taken his weapons. Eagle had asked, but had received only the noncommittal grunt which had become so familiar.

He stepped to the ledge and straightened to his full height. Sun Boy was painting the western sky with his brilliant colors. Only a few smoky blue clouds broke the expanse of orange and pink, and even those clouds were edged with a splash of color. Sun Boy was at his best tonight, thought Eagle, as he started down the ledge.

He gingerly stepped along the narrow part of the path, past the jumble of boulders, and was nearing the final, easier portion of the descent, when he saw a motion in the trees across the river. He stopped, almost in midstride, and carefully studied the area. There was no further sign, and Eagle had almost decided that he was mistaken. Then, a budding branch swayed slightly, as if in a breeze. But there was no breeze.

All his attention now concentrated on that particular section of the dogwood thicket. It could be no more than a wandering deer, but he must be sure. Carefully, he lowered himself to a sitting position to watch. He cast an anxious glance at the fading western sky. There was not much time, and he could not continue his plan to leave the sanctuary of the cave until he was certain he was not observed.

The light was practically gone when he saw the next motion. Eagle had realized that in a sense he had the advantage over the watcher. He, Eagle, could move, relax, change his position, be comfortable, because he was already under observation. The other, if indeed there were anyone there, must conceal himself, remain unmoving.

Eagle concentrated on the pain the watcher must be feeling, the cramp of tense muscles, caught in an unnatural position. He could all but feel the presence of the man, clumsily hidden behind the thin screen of the dogwood thicket. So, it came as no surprise when the movement came.

Eagle was looking directly at the spot when a moccasined foot shifted slightly. Within a few heartbeats, he had made out the vague outline of a crouching warrior. One of the younger members of the party, no doubt, assigned to watch and report. This would account for the man's lack of finesse, his failure to carry out his assignment without being discovered.

Now, there would be no problem. Eagle would wait for full darkness, finish the descent, and kill the watcher before he departed. He leaned against the warm stone and relaxed to wait.

Eagle was almost ready to continue his plan when another thought occurred to him. If the young warrior had been assigned to watch, he would have been expected to report any attempt to leave the cave. And it would be necessary to carry the message to the camp of the others. That would leave the cave unobserved. There was only one possible way for the enemy to deal with this problem. There must be two watchers below.

Of course. There would be one older, experienced warrior and the young man on his first scouting party. One could continue the watch while the other carried the message. Eagle had no inkling where the other man might be hidden and could not risk descent in the darkness.

Reluctantly, he turned back up the path to the cave. He would have to devise another plan.

CHAPTER 26

Some time after darkness had fallen, the two Head Splitter scouts moved cautiously to a place where they could talk.

"You must be more careful, Red Sky," spoke the older man. "He saw you move."

"No, I think not," the younger retorted, a trifle irritated. "He just came down, sat for a while, and went back."

The older man chuckled mirthlessly. The man they observed, the one called Broken Leg, was far more clever than he appeared. His demeanor as a prisoner had been deceptive and had fooled most of the party. Perhaps even Bull's Tail himself, though one would not say so aloud.

The capabilities of the prisoner had become apparent when the real-bear charged. The captive had fled into the night, making his escape in the confusion. The man had courage, too, to wander in the darkness with the wounded real-bear prowling and splashing in the stream. As they had read the trail next morning, at times the tracks seemed so close that the fugitive and the bear appeared to be traveling together.

Then there was the death of Gray Fox. He had been perhaps their best tracker and had followed the trail of the fugitive alone. It must have been near the coming of daylight that he met his end, mauled horribly by the real-bear.

There was much not easily understood. Someone had taken the weapons of Gray Fox, presumably the fleeing Broken Leg. But, again, how had the man escaped the real-bear?

Bull's Tail insisted that the fugitive must have companions. The war party had scouted thoroughly, but had seen no one. It was true, at times the trail appeared as if there were two fleeing men. One was undoubtedly Broken Leg, his tracks marked by a decided limp where he had come from the stream and walked a few paces in the soft earth.

No one had seen the other man. There had even been an argument over one section of the trail. What appeared to be the track of a second man was unclear, smudged and trampled by both that of Broken Leg and that of the bear. There was a spatter of blood, and it was thought for a time that the wounded bear was tracking the fleeing man or men. But the bear had not been seen again, and its trail had been lost.

Bull's Tail had been furious at the clever way that the fleeing Broken Leg had maneuvered upwind and fired the prairie grass. The war party had been hard pressed to start backfires and reach a place of safety. In the midst of the milling confusion, someone had pointed to a distant ridge.

"Look!"

There, through the shifting smoke and leaping orange flame, could be seen the figure of their quarry, standing on the hill to watch their confusion. Or were there two figures on the crest of the ridge? Again, argument ensued. No one could be sure, as the shimmering waves of heat from the fire distorted the distant scene.

Finally, Bull's Tail had had enough.

"Crow! You and Red Sky follow them! Find where they go!"

The scouts found a circuitous route around and through the fire and moved their horses in the general direction taken by the fugitives. Crow had repeatedly had to caution the enthusiastic young Red Sky.

"Remember, they are on foot. We move faster. Be careful."

They saw a track from time to time. Crow was still not certain whether they were following one man or two.

By the time darkness had fallen, it was apparent that Broken Leg was heading toward the bluff where he had been captured. Crow pointed ahead.

"He must have a cave there."

The two left their horses, hobbled, in a meadow with good grass and water and moved ahead on foot. It was fully dark when they arrived at the river below the bluff, moving carefully to observe without being seen. It was much later, even, when Crow noticed a dim glow near the top of the rock. The light flickered, muted, soft, but the significance was certain. In a cave high above, the fugitive had built a small fire for warmth.

This discovery explained many things. This shelter had enabled Broken Leg to survive the winter. Perhaps his story was true, after all, and he was alone.

The two had concealed themselves and waited through the night, chilled to the bone, envying their quarry the warmth of the fire. Not until the sun was well up had Broken Leg emerged from the cave.

They had watched through the day and saw that the man moved about, apparently unaware that he was observed. Evening was near when Broken Leg prepared to descend. Now, for the first time, the watchers could see the narrow ledge by which he had reached the cave.

Crow was disappointed when the man became suspicious. He was certain that the impatient Red Sky had shifted position at the wrong moment. Ah, well, it was no matter. They had scouted well. They could report to their chief the location of the cave and that there was only one man. At least, Crow thought so.

"You have seen only the one man?"

Red Sky nodded.

"He came down that path along a ledge of some sort and then went back."

Crow was mildly irritated at his companion. Red Sky was not the most intelligent of the younger warriors. It was like him to restate the obvious. Crow had felt some resentment at being paired with one so inept but had accepted it with dignity. After all, it did show his chief's confidence in the ability of Crow.

Now Crow had an idea.

"Red Sky, I will watch here. You go and tell the chief what we have found."

The younger man was eager. It would be much more comfortable to travel, to arrive at the camp of the war party, than to huddle half frozen for another night. Quickly, he gathered himself and departed at a swinging trot, thinking of the warm fire ahead.

Now Crow was alone. He had always worked well alone. He had a very clear idea of the path to the cave. He had noted carefully the portion where the fugitive had seemed most cautious. That would be the narrow portion, the part for extreme care. No matter, one could feel one's way on all fours in the darkness.

For Crow intended to climb to the cave. He was a much braver and more skilled warrior than he had ever received credit for. Now he had an opportunity to show his ability. Alone, he would capture or kill the enemy in his own lair. For this, there would be many honors. The name of Crow would be sung around the dance fires for many summers.

He checked his weapons and placed his robe aside with his bow and arrows. After some thought, his war club was added to the pile. There might be no room to swing such a weapon. It would be best to rely on his knife.

Crow looked up and down the river, a last evaluation of the night, before he began his mission. A great owl called from the woods, and another answered from somewhere on the face of the bluff. Otherwise, all was quiet except for the song of the water over the shallows. Crow took a deep breath and waded into the icy water.

He had some idea of the breadth and depth. He had seen Broken Leg swim across. Therefore, he was not surprised when the river's bottom shelved off sharply, and he began to swim, making as little noise as possible. Carefully, he hauled himself up on the narrow strip of shore at the bottom of the cliff. In the dimness of the faint starlight, Crow began to inspect the face of the bluff. Ah, yes, there it was, to his left, almost hidden behind a fringe of willows. The ledge rose above the level of the bar, clinging to the sheer face of the wall.

He could see little, and it was mostly by feel that Crow crept slowly up the path, hugging the still sun-warmed face of the rock. He was exultant. The fugitive would never expect an enemy to scale the bluff in the dead of night. And even without the element of surprise, Crow had no serious doubts as to his ability to conquer the other. He had seen the weakness, the ineptness of the man called Broken Leg. The fugitive might be clever, yes, but no match for Crow in combat. He crept on, upward along the shelf.

It was nearly halfway, as he approached the jumble of boulders, that Crow became apprehensive. The dim shapes in the starlight became living shadows, shapes from nightmares, fearsome creatures from some Spirit-World.

Crow, who had never feared the darkness, stopped, confused. He studied the shapeless forms, and they became only a jumble of rocks again. His confidence returned. He had only to make certain that no enemy lurked there. At length he assured himself and moved forward.

For only a moment a shudder passed across the back of his shoulders. He recalled that the soul of a warrior killed in combat in the time of darkness must wander homeless forever. He shrugged away the thought. He, Crow, would not be the one to die tonight. He moved ahead, among the rocks, made more confident by their warm smooth surfaces as he touched them in passing.

Now came the narrow part of the trail, and Crow dropped to all fours to creep forward. Somehow the feeling of dread assailed him again. It was as if someone watched, unseen. Not the man he stalked, but someone, or something, else. There was the overwhelming feeling of another presence, some medicine spirit of great strength.

Confused, Crow's resolve weakened. He would have retreated, but dared not try to turn around on all fours on the narrow ledge. Sweating in spite of the cold, he crept forward. To his right, a darker shadow with a fringe of growth indicated a rift or cleft in the rock. His extended hand contacted a stick, jutting across the path. Cautiously, he tested the growth. It might be merely a bush, clinging to a precarious footing in the cleft, but it might be a trap. A clever fugitive could have constructed a deadfall. To move the slender stick might bring rocks crashing down in the dark. Momentarily, Crow wondered why he had ever attempted this climb. He paused, indecisive, wishing to retreat. Carefully, he rose to his feet to turn around and move back down the path.

In the distance, the hunting owl called. Crow was completely unprepared for the answering call. It was close beside him, at arm's length, from the narrow crevice. Startled, Crow stepped back and his foot slipped from the ledge. As he fell, he was aware of the quiet swish of great wings past his head.

A gasp was the only sound from the falling warrior as he plummeted downward. He had hardly realized what had happened before he crashed into the branches of a great sycamore below. His neck and back were wrenched backward, forcibly distorting the anatomy.

The crumpled form hung in the branches, twitching slightly for a few moments before it became limp. Slowly it slid free and dropped heavily into the dark water below.

CHAPTER 27

Bull's Tail and the war party arrived at the river before day-light. At first, he had been irked at being roused from his bed. But Red Sky was insistent.

The urgency, it seemed, was that the man they sought had attempted to leave the area. He had descended the bluff carry-ing a pack and a walking staff.

In the end, Bull's Tail decided that if Crow thought the cir-cumstances important enough to send a message, it would be well to move. Thus, the war party assembled quietly and trav-eled to the spot indicated by Red Sky.

The first inkling that something was wrong came when they could find no sign of Crow. The warriors dispersed, moving up and down the river, searching quietly as the thinning darkness was replaced by gray dawn.

Then, as visibility improved, someone summoned the chief, and led him almost to the spot where they had first seen the lone warrior. There lay the robe of the missing Crow. It was folded carefully and placed against the base of a tree. Just as carefully, Crow's weapons were arranged on the folded robe.

Now the hair prickled on the back of the chief's neck. What strange things were happening? Nothing, it seemed, had moved in an orderly fashion for this war party. From the time they had first seen the stranger bathing in the river, the entire expedition had rapidly crumbled in decay. It was as if some-thing strange and unnatural was at work.

Of course, Bull's Tail had recognized the eccentric behavior of the prisoner for what it was, an attempt at diversion. That was no matter, though he was disturbed by the reactions of his young warriors. They did not take this man as seriously as they should. Perhaps they had learned that by now.

The real turning point, when the expedition began to turn to dung before his very eyes, had been the matter of the real-bear. His most capable warrior had been killed, the prisoner had escaped, and by Sun's rising, they had lost their best tracker. There was the added insult that the escaped prisoner had outwitted them twice, once passing their camp in the night by wading the river and again by firing the prairie. Bull's Tail was still certain that the fugitive had a companion, perhaps more than one.

Perhaps, with all the strange happenings, they should abandon the war party and go home. Already, the sweet taste of triumph over capturing an important subchief of the Elk-dog People had turned to bitter gall in his mouth.

Just then there was a shout from downstream. Angrily, Bull's Tail wheeled and started in that direction. Someone was in need of a reprimand for breaking the silence. Then he relented. What did it matter? The entire war party had become a disaster anyway. Their medicine was bad. He was certain that the fugitive in the cave was already aware of all their movements. He was working up a massive hate for this man.

He pushed through the fringe of the thicket and elbowed aside a warrior or two. The group was standing, hushed and tense, as they stared at a twisted shape in the water.

The open eyes of Crow stared sightlessly at the sky through the shallow water of the sandbar where his body had lodged. His neck was broken, and the expression frozen on the dead face seemed a strange mixture of confusion and terror.

Again, for an instant, Bull's Tail had the eerie feeling that he was dealing with things beyond his understanding. He experienced an emotion very close to fear. How could one deal with a medicine that was mysteriously destroying his most trusted warriors one by one?

Fortunately, at that moment the sun's first rays shone through the budding trees. With the broad light of day, things always appear more favorable.

It was pure coincidence, Bull's Tail decided, that the party had been attacked by the real-bear. Of course, the most aggressive warriors had been those killed. Two of their horses had run away in the darkness to be lost. But were not elk-dogs always afraid of a bear?

And Crow? He had apparently attempted to climb the bluff in the dark. It was logical, though unfortunate, that he had fallen to his death. It had been a matter of poor judgment.

Now Bull's Tail needed something to shake his followers out of their numb, half-fearful daze. Perhaps he could use the death of Crow to his advantage.

"We will avenge our brother," he muttered.

Almost instantly, the desired effect was seen. From a hushed, fearful group emerged an angry spirit of vengeance. Crow had never been popular. He had been much too haughty, but now everyone remembered him as a trusted friend.

"Death to the slayer of Crow!" someone shouted.

Bull's Tail would have preferred capture and ransom, but this solution would be an acceptable compromise. It would provide a diversion for his warriors. It would be better than allowing them to slip into the sort of negative feelings that he had felt himself. Bull's Tail had not become a respected leader of men without being able to read their feelings.

"Avenge Crow's death!" he added and smiled inwardly at the responding shout.

Men lifted the body of Crow from the river, to prepare for burial. Others moved back along the stream to search for the path to the cave.

"It must be near where we first saw him," called Bull's Tail.

Two young men plunged into the water to swim across. The chief stood, hands on hips, watching. He meticulously examined every fragment of stone and scrubby growth on the opposite bluff.

"Red Sky! Where did you see the cave?"

The young warrior came to his chief's elbow and pointed. "There."

Bull's Tail still could see no opening. Only by careful direction from young Red Sky was it possible to determine even the general area. In the course of things, even Red Sky, who had seen the cave, became confused. The bluff had looked far different in the dark. Had the fire's glow come from behind that clump of brush, or the other, the one on the left?

Bull's Tail impatiently waved him aside. It did not matter. There must be a path, a trail to reach the hiding place. They would find it.

When they did, they would attack. Even in a protected hiding place, what chance did one lone man have? They could starve him out if necessary. But, Bull's Tail thought, it would be better to mount a massive attack on the fugitive's cave. That would allow the young men to vent their emotions.

Another thought occurred to him. They should be certain that there was no other path, no escape to the top of the bluff. Quickly, he summoned two warriors and explained the strategy. They must move upstream until they came to a place where they could climb the bluff. Then they would move back to this area. He pointed to a large dead tree, which had toppled partially over the edge of the rim. That could be a landmark. With warriors to block his escape above, the fugitive would be trapped on the bluff's face, between the two groups of the war party.

Yes, Bull's Tail told himself, this might yet become a day with good medicine. This good feeling was reinforced by a shout from across the river. The scouts had located the path.

CHAPTER 28

Eagle had remained alert after it became apparent that he was watched. He sat in the cave entrance, wrapped in his robe against the chill of the night, and listened. Vague sounds below told of some activity, but when he heard someone cross the river and start up the path, Eagle knew he must act.

It would be best, he felt, to accost the climbers at the narrow portion of the ledge. He took his walking staff and slipped quietly along the path until he found the proper spot. There he flattened himself against the wall, staff ready. He could deliver a deadly blow to the attacker, who would be attempting to maintain his balance on the treacherous shelf. There might be time for only one swing of the staff, but it could be the only one needed.

It seemed like half the night before the enemy warrior could be heard approaching. By leaning forward, Eagle could see him at a little distance in the dim starlight, threading through the broken boulders halfway down the path. The man seemed hesitant, and Eagle sensed the fear in his attitude. Then he seemed to regain confidence and moved forward again.

The attacker dropped to all fours as he came to the narrow portion of the ledge. That was sensible, in unfamiliar terrain in the dark.

There was a short stretch of the path which was out of sight from Eagle's position. A slight bulge in the rock obscured his view. Eagle readied himself, knowing that his next glimpse of the enemy would bring him close enough to strike. He poised, waiting.

In the distance, he heard the hunting owl's call and the answer very close at hand. There was a startled gasp from the unseen enemy warrior, and Eagle caught the merest glimpse of the falling body as the man went over the edge. The owl, startled from its nesting crevice, swept past on silent wings. Eagle listened, hearing the sickening crash into the sycamore and a long moment later the muffled splash. Then silence.

The odd thought struck Eagle that perhaps the Old Man had been involved in this incident. His better judgment rejected the thought. The warrior had merely tried a difficult climb in unfamiliar terrain and in the dark had fallen.

The more urgent question was, were there more warriors coming up the path behind this one? Eagle watched for some time, but finally decided not. He had reasoned that there were only two scouts, and one had made the attempt at the bluff. The other would be needed to carry the message to the party's leader. Perhaps he had already gone to bring the others.

Now Eagle faced an important decision. If he remained here, the entire enemy war party would soon arrive. It was a very defensible place, but Eagle had the typical plainsman's uneasiness of closed places. If he must fight for his life, it might be better to do so in the open, under the broad sky, than hiding in a hole. This vague feeling was the basis for his decision. There would be no better time to leave than now, before the Head Splitters arrived in force, before they discovered the body in the river.

Quickly, he lifted his pack again and began the descent. Eagle hated to make the descent in the dark. He disliked heights at best and was much more content on more gently rolling ground. It was almost easier, however, not to be able to see the trees, rocks, and water below. He cautiously felt his way along, pausing to make certain the owl would not startle him into reacting as the hapless Head Splitter had done. The owl was nowhere to be seen, and he moved ahead.

He paused for a rest among the boulders and listened for

any chance sound that would indicate the presence of the enemy. He heard nothing.

Moving on, he reached the narrow bar at the river's edge. Here, he must be very cautious. He would be extremely vulnerable as he emerged from the river on the other side. If even one enemy lay in the shadows over there, this could be a fateful moment.

At long last, Eagle satisfied himself that there was no one watching from the other shore. He took a last glance at the Seven Hunters to see how much darkness remained and stepped into the chill of the river. Water rose slowly past his knees with the first few steps, as he gingerly felt his way into the deeper channel. His pack was held above his head to avoid wetting his food supply. A quick plunge would have been an easier and faster way to cross, but he could not do so with his burden. Besides, he wished to be as quiet as possible in case there were enemies in the woods.

The water rose to his groin, and he tightened his muscles against its icy clutch at his tender parts. At any moment now, he would step off the ledge into the deep current. He felt his way forward.

It was fortunate, perhaps, that he had not yet begun to swim, when there was a soft movement in the narrow strip of trees. From his low vantage point at the water's surface, Eagle could see silhouetted against the night sky the forms of several warriors. One was unmistakably the burly form of Bull's Tail. The entire war party had returned, and Eagle's attempt to leave was too late.

Eagle realized that now his survival must depend on his silence. He must move very slowly and above all do no splashing. Carefully he turned and waded back toward the shore. His progress seemed painfully slow, and at any moment he expected a shout of discovery, probably to be followed by a shower of arrows at his unprotected back.

Finally he stepped to the shore. The trickle of water dripping from his soaked garments seemed loud enough to wake the dead, but was apparently unheard. He moved swiftly to the path and began his climb. In the eastern sky behind him, the gray false dawn was beginning to prepare the way for Sun Boy. There was very little time for Eagle to reach concealment. If he were discovered on the ledge, he would be within easy bowshot of the enemy. Still, he must not move too fast. The motion itself might attract enemy eyes. Daylight was growing rapidly.

He had not quite reached the sheltering screen of brush before the cave mouth when there was a shout from below. For a moment, Eagle thought he had been discovered. He flattened on the ledge and peered between the dogwood stems. But the excitement was moving in another direction. Men were moving downstream, gathering at the riffle. As the light improved, Eagle could see the enemy warriors standing in shallow water, looking at something in the stream. Then he realized. They had discovered the body of their scout.

He continued to watch. Bull's Tail elbowed his way forward, and there was a brief period of hushed, almost fearful discussion. Eagle saw the first rays from Sun Boy's torch probe through the thin timber, beyond the cluster of enemy warriors. Then, as if that were a signal, there came a shout. Eagle could not understand the words in the enemies' tongue, but the meaning was clear. There was a new tone of determination, of vengeance, in the shouts of the men who ran searching up and down the stream.

Bull's Tail stalked to a point almost opposite the cave, talking and pointing. At one time, Eagle was certain that he was seen, as the burly chief looked and pointed directly at him. Then their line of vision moved on.

More threatening was the fact that now two men splashed into the river and swam across to the narrow bar against the bluff. Eagle knew it would take no time for them to discover the path. In fact, he may have led them to discover it. The wet trail of dripping water he had left would lead the searchers directly to the partially concealed ledge behind the willows.

He had hardly realized this alarming fact when the shout came from below. Eagle had no doubt as to its meaning. The two warriors were shouting to the others that they had discovered the path.

CHAPTER 29

Another two warriors splashed across the river to the base of the bluff, while still others gathered directly across on the shore opposite the cave. Eagle knew that his best opportunity to stop the attackers was again at the narrow ledge. He must return to that spot.

There was one other thing. He could not do so without being seen by the warriors across the river. So, since the attackers already knew of his presence, Eagle decided to take advantage of the situation. Rather than make the futile effort to sneak down the path unnoticed, he would attempt a spectacular move.

He stood to his full height, boldly exposing himself to the enemy. A shout of triumph came from below, and men pointed upward to the figure on the ledge. Eagle decided to continue the ludicrous characterization he had begun previously. He shouted, but knowing they would not understand his tongue, accompanied his words with sign talk.

"Who disturbs the sleep of Broken Leg?" he demanded.

He was answered by a chorus of howls and threats.

"The Head Splitters do not know the meaning of proper talk," he returned. "You do not behave as guests should when meeting at the lodge of a chief."

There were indignant hoots of anger and outrage, and a few obscene gestures. An arrow, nearly spent, struck against the bluff and fell to the ledge. Eagle picked it up, examined it casually, and tossed it carelessly in the direction of the attackers.

"Here, little one! Try again! You must practice much before you are a warrior! Here is your target!"

He stood haughtily, thrusting his chest forward, daring them to waste their arrows. He paced up and down the ledge, occasionally stopping to spread arms wide and point to the center of his breast.

"Son of a dog!" screamed one of the younger warriors, with accompanying gestures. "We will use your dead body for practice!"

"Do rabbits hunt real-bears?" Eagle retorted. "Who will make your kill? I see no warriors."

Now Bull's Tail stepped forward. He motioned the others to silence.

"Broken Leg!" he called. "You know you cannot escape. Come down, and I will spare your life."

"*Aiee!*" Eagle hooted. "Your mother eats dung! How many men have you lost, Bull's Tail? Who is next to die?"

There was a moment of pause before the answering chorus of angry shouts, and Eagle knew that his thrust had struck home. True, he could not personally take credit for any of the fallen warriors, but he could make them think. He knew that the war party was suffering an unacceptably high number of casualties, with nothing whatever to show for it.

Furious, Bull's Tail seized the bow from a young man next to him and launched a shot at the defiant figure above. Eagle watched closely and was able to step casually aside to avoid the shaft. It shattered harmlessly beside him.

"*Aiee!*" Eagle taunted. "You are no better than your young men!"

He had been watching the path from the corner of his eye and seen the warriors start to climb. Timing would be important now.

Almost carelessly, he stepped quickly along the ledge and scuttled to the point where the bulge of the bluff concealed him from the climbers. He was none too soon. A moccasined foot extended carefully around the blind spot on the path. Without waiting, Eagle swung the heavy staff with all his strength. He felt the snap of bone under the blow and heard a surprised cry of pain. He had thought that the man might go over the edge, but he apparently regained his balance on the narrow shelf. There was excited conversation around the corner and the sounds of the injured man being dragged backward by the others.

There were shouts from below, and an arrow shattered against the rock. Splinters struck Eagle's cheek, and he realized that it had been a near miss. He could not stay in this spot. The range was shorter than when he had stood in front of the cave, and sooner or later, a bowman would loose a lucky shot. He must find another place, one not so vulnerable, from which to stop the attackers.

He scuttled back along the shelf and noticed as he passed a dead plum bush beside the trail. If only he could build a barrier of some sort to slow the advance. He recalled that in the stories of his childhood, the People had once defended themselves for an entire winter with a massive barrier of brush across a narrow meadow. It had served well until the enemy had burned the barrier.

The idea of a brush barrier remained in his mind. True, the enemy could push such an obstacle from the ledge as fast as he could replace it. There was not enough dry growth, anyway, for more than a temporary deterrent.

But what if it were on fire? The attackers could not approach closely enough to push it over the edge, without bringing long poles from below. Quickly he checked the breeze. Yes, it would carry the smoke and flame toward the enemy.

Eagle gathered a handful of dry grass and wrenched a few stems from the dead plum thicket. Back down the trail, he selected his most favorable spot and arranged the twigs and grass. Hurrying back to the cave, he picked a glowing stick from the fire and started back down the path. Then he had an amusing thought.

"Bull's Tail!" he shouted and signed, "I have enjoyed the visit, but now I really must cook my dinner. Will you join me?"

Boldly, he stalked back along the path and thrust his firebrand into the dry tinder. The slight breeze fanned the coals into open flame, and smoke began to drift along the face of the bluff. Eagle moved back and forth, dodging an occasional arrow, adding twigs and branches to the crackling fire, now completely blocking the narrow ledge.

With a great show of boldness, he opened his pack and took out strips of meat. He sat near his fire to eat, merely to infuriate his attackers further.

Eagle did not deceive himself. His situation was desperate. The fuel available to keep the fire alive on the ledge was limited. Likewise, he had only one small skin of water. He was at risk from the bowmen at all times.

In fact, Eagle had decided that this might well be his day to die. He could die well, taking a number of the enemy with him. And he could do better if he could keep the enemy angry, frustrated, off balance. They would be more vulnerable.

Eagle rose, yawned, and rubbed his stomach with satisfaction. He tipped the waterskin and made a great display of drinking long and deep, as if he had water to spare. Actually, he was drinking very little, only holding the skin so as to appear to be using the precious fluid wastefully.

He sauntered lazily back up to the cave and broke an armful of branches from the dead tree, still balanced on the ledge. He had utilized most of the easily reached smaller branches already and now was breaking some of the larger limbs as he was able. Above him, he saw a branch just out of reach, with excellent fuel to offer. He stepped up on one of the more substantial limbs, which rested its broken tip on the ledge, and an idea struck him. Could he climb to the top of the bluff on this inverted trunk?

Without changing his original intent, Eagle broke off the twigs and carried them along the ledge to a point near the fire. There were a few jeers and a poorly aimed arrow, but the enemy was largely quiet. They seemed content to wait. Very well, he could do the same.

There was enough fuel to last the day, and in the darkness he might climb to safety. He stretched on his back on the ledge before the cave to study the big tree. The possibility looked very good. He could start at the east side, then halfway up, work his way across to the right. The difficult part would be the last short way along the thick part of the trunk. There would be the stubs of broken roots above him, with dirt and rocks intertwined. He believed that he could reach high over head and pull himself up with his arms.

While thinking of these things, Eagle fell asleep. It seemed an unlikely time and place, but he was exhausted from loss of sleep the past two nights. He dreamed troubled, fragmented pictures of himself climbing, slowly, painfully, unable quite to reach the next branch. Meanwhile an insolent squirrel ran up and down and around him, scolding at his intrusion.

He woke, and the scolding voice of the squirrel was real. The creature sat above him and chattered indignantly. Eagle smiled and rose. His fire was dying down on the ledge, and he hastened to build it up again, taking care to wave a cheerful greeting to the watching enemy on the other shore.

He would wait until darkness to try his escape.

CHAPTER 30

It was difficult to be patient, to wait until darkness. Eagle spent the time leisurely moving up and down the ledge, keeping his fire tended and exchanging occasional obscenities with the Head Splitters. They had all but stopped shooting arrows at him. No prudent warrior would continue to waste his weapons on the chance of a lucky shot.

Eagle became increasingly convinced that his plan would work. In his mind's eye, he made the climb a hundred times. He could almost feel the sensation as he stepped the last high step with his left foot and reached with his hand for the root above him.

When Sun Boy finally retired, Eagle built up both the fire on the ledge and that in the cave. He moved back and forth to establish his presence, and when it seemed the time was right, approached the tree.

For the first few moments, the climb was easy. When he moved sideways to the right, things became more difficult. He longed for the agility of a spider scuttling sideways on its web. At one point, he simply could not find his next handhold. There must be one. He had seen it from the ledge. But his grasping left hand encountered only empty space. He could not reach the limb. It would be necessary for him to loose his grip with his right hand and make a blind grab in the dark. Eagle wondered, if his grasp missed, whether he would fall merely to the ledge or over the edge to the river below. Cold sweat beaded on his forehead and trickled down between his shoulder blades. He longed to relax, to rest his aching muscles.

Well, he must do something even if it was wrong. Taking a

deep breath, he let go his grasp and made a sweeping grab in the darkness with his left hand. The wrist banged painfully into the sought-for limb, and his fingers closed over it as he swung dangerously before regaining his balance.

Most alarming, though, was the subtle shift of the position of the tree under him. It was small, hardly worth notice, except for the thing it implied. The tree was, at best, balanced precariously on the ledge. It would take only a slight rotation, a small change in the delicate balance, to let the entire trunk of the dead giant slide over the edge.

Frantic, Eagle closed his eyes against the shower of dirt and small stones that pattered down on him from above. He hung helpless, trying not to move or shift his weight. After what seemed an endless time, the shifting looseness under him ceased. Now, Eagle knew, he must go ahead. Carefully, he pulled himself upward, trying to make no sudden moves. Hand over hand, foot following foot, hugging the rough bark of the trunk in places that offered no handhold, he crept upward. He could see the sprawl of the broken roots above him now, almost within reach. He had not realized the extent of their overhang. He would nearly be forced to bend backward to slither over the final barrier.

Eagle felt above him, and loose dirt fell again. Perhaps he could dislodge enough to make a better place to climb over, or between, the spreading roots. He found a solid grasp and, working with the other hand, began to claw away the dirt. Soon he could reach through and lock his elbow around a massive root. Relieved somewhat, he hung there to rest. Slowly the numbed muscles of his hand began to return to normal, and he was able to reevaluate his position.

Far below, he could see the flickering campfires of the enemy and closer the glow of his own barrier fire on the ledge. He looked up at the open night sky and allowed his eyes to adjust from the bright points of firelight to the dim starlight along the bluff rim.

To his surprise, Eagle discovered that he was actually

slightly higher than the level of the rim. The roots of the great tree had heaved upward as the giant fell, and he was forced to climb over the highest point of the tangled roots or to move around to a better position.

Anxiously, he poked more dirt away in an effort to see through, to try to decide the best course of action. He placed his eye to the space between two of the spreading roots and recoiled in alarm. Only a few paces away, a tiny campfire burned. Two men were seated there. He was surprised that they had not heard him during the climb.

The next shock almost caused Eagle to lose his grasp and fall backward entirely. It was a whisper, out of the darkness directly in front of him. In the hollow formed by the tearing away of the root cluster sat a familiar figure, comfortably at ease.

"We must go back down," said the Old Man calmly. "They are already here."

Eagle felt later that, had he not been so furious at the old recluse, he would never have had the strength to make the difficult descent. To make matters worse, the Old Man had slipped easily over the tangled roots and was following Eagle closely down the trunk. Dirt, dislodged stones, and pieces of bark kept pattering down on Eagle's head. He felt that, if he were too slow, the Old Man would at any moment step on his fingers. Once more, he marveled at the agility of the wiry old man.

Eagle dropped the last short distance to the ledge and fell panting and sweating. Anger washed through his mouth in a dry, bitter taste. The Old Man could surely have warned him before he had exhausted himself in the useless climb. He could almost feel more hate for his companion than for the enemies below, waiting to kill them both. He could hardly stand the sight and smell of the repulsive old creature.

The Old Man was calmly poking around the cave. He picked up Eagle's pack.

"Do you have any meat?"

Eagle laughed. How could he remain angry at the ludicrous old figure, who, after all, may have just saved his life once again? The two sat down and chewed meat together.

"Where have you been, Uncle?"

It was well that Eagle did not really expect an answer, because he was not likely to receive one. The Old Man merely grunted and made a vague gesture at the night.

Eagle started to relate the events since they last parted, but decided not to. The other could ask if he wished. Besides, Eagle somehow had the feeling that the Old Man already knew everything that had gone on in the vicinity. He even wondered if the oldster knew of another, a secret path, up and down this rock. Then he shook his head, puzzled. What a strange thought.

The Old Man went through his ritual. He yawned, belched, scratched his groin, and lay down.

"Sleep!" he said simply. "We have much to do tomorrow."

The words were hardly from his lips before they were followed by a resonant snore.

With a mixture of resentment and amusement, Eagle went to tend the fire on the ledge and stood for a moment looking across the dark prairie. Below him shone the glow of dying campfires. He wondered if Bull's Tail slept, or if he lay sleepless, planning what would surely be the final assault on the fugitives in the cave.

Bull's Tail was awake, staring at the fire on the cliff. There was still something strange happening, he felt. The lone fugitive (he had now decided there was only one) was clever and resourceful, but his days had run out. Yet, the man was so resourceful, his medicine so strong. He had earned the admiration and respect of Bull's Tail. It might be better simply to leave and let the man go.

Actually, that would have been the chief's preference at this point. But it would never do. He had used the situation to arouse the fighting ardor of his young men. The other man had helped admirably with his clever insults from the bluff.

No, let the young men make their kill. It would make better warriors of them.

CHAPTER 31

The first attack came shortly after daylight. Eagle had realized that he was faced with a losing battle when his fuel began to dwindle. He had kept the fire on the ledge alive through the night, fully realizing that it was highly unlikely that an attempt would come in the dark. So he had carefully nurtured the coals, adding just enough twigs to keep a good spirit of life in the warm ashes.

Now, as sunlight burned the mists of fog from the trees along the river, Eagle saw a flurry of determined activity in the enemy camp. Three bowmen arrayed themselves at the opposite shore, and a similar number of warriors crossed the river again to begin the climb up the ledge.

Eagle piled the last of his fuel on the embers and fanned the twigs into flame. An arrow struck near him as he crouched and retreated back up the ledge to a safer vantage point.

Bull's Tail stood on the opposite shore.

"Broken Leg!" he called. "You must come down now or be killed."

"Who would kill me?" shouted Eagle. "I am Eagle, son of Heads Off, of the Elk-dog band. Is an eagle to be killed by carrion eaters?"

They might as well remember the name of their adversary, he reasoned. He intended for them to remember this day for the rest of their lives.

Eagle glanced down the path at his fire and saw that the worst had happened. The attackers had brought a long pole up the trail and, from the safety of the bluff's bulge, were pushing at the fire. Helpless, he watched as the pole relentlessly shoved blazing branches to the edge and over. He could hear the rattle of the burning sticks as they struck the trees below and then the quick, steamy hiss as they dropped to the water. Quickly the ledge was cleared.

Eagle hurried down the path and readied his staff as before. He half-crouched to present a smaller target for the arrows that were now beginning to strike around him. Devoutly he hoped that the bowmen were not the most accurate shots among the Head Splitters. So far he was untouched.

It was only a short while until Eagle saw, as before, a moccasined foot slide cautiously around the corner. Again, he swung a bone-crushing blow with his staff. No sooner had the staff struck than he realized he had been duped. The texture of the leg was wrong. Instead of the solid feel of flesh and bone, there was a softness in the object of his blow. The enemy had extended, on a stick, a moccasin and legging stuffed with dried grass. Too late, he felt the grasp of hands on the other end of his staff.

Eagle braced himself for the pull, muscles straining. He could see only an occasional glimpse of his adversary around the bulging corner of stone, as they struggled for possession of the weapon. He was a rugged, heavyset man with bulging shoulders and arms like those of a bear. There were shouts from below, where the warriors on the other side could see the entire contest.

There was little time to think, as the struggle continued. Both men were striving to hug as closely to the wall as possible. Eagle's tired muscles began to cramp, and he concentrated on how his opponent must feel. What would happen, he wondered, when the staff slipped from the other man's grasp? Would he, Eagle, slip from the ledge as he fell backward? No sooner had the thought crossed his mind than he knew the answer. In a heartbeat's time, Eagle relaxed his pull and thrust heavily forward and outward. The end of the staff jerked forcibly away, leaving Eagle weaponless. He had only a brief glimpse of the man's surprised face as the other struck forcibly on his back and right shoulder and bounced into emptiness, still clutching the staff.

Quickly, Eagle drew his knife and stood waiting. There was no immediate further attack, but a shout and a shower of arrows from below warned him to withdraw. He retreated partway up the trail and stopped at his next vantage point.

He regretted the loss of the staff, but was pleased at the same time. He had considered tying his knife to the staff as a rude spear. How fortunate that he had not done so. He would have been completely weaponless. Now, at least, he would have his knife with which to face one attacker at a time on the ledge.

The enemy would probably be armed with war clubs, possibly knives also. He doubted that any would carry a bow. It would be clumsy to use in the limited space on the ledge. Besides, the best bowmen would be below, shooting when opportunity offered.

Mentally, he counted the Head Splitters he must face. There had been fourteen originally in the party. Two had been killed by the bear, another had fallen from the bluff in the dark. The man with the broken ankle would be out of action and so would the one who had just fallen. That would leave nine, counting the two at the clifftop. He could see three bowmen and Bull's Tail himself below. *Aiee*, there could be no more than three on the ledge!

"Bull's Tail!" he taunted, standing so that his sign talk might be easily seen. "How many men have you now?"

Eagle felt, unaccountably, as if he had a definite advantage. Only three men to meet on the ledge, to meet one at a time. He was feeling the old excitement of competition. He now felt capable of hand-to-hand combat and was ready to take all comers.

Yet, the thing which had made Eagle a successful warrior

was not merely sheer strength and agility. He had realized, while still quite young, that it was unnecessary to expend brute force if cleverness would suffice. Now, it would be well to use all the cleverness he could muster and save his strength for the final onslaught. Already, he could see that the attackers were guilty of not planning well. They could easily wait him out, wait until his water was exhausted. Instead, they were choosing the more dangerous route, direct attack on a difficult position.

Bull's Tail was shouting again.

"Broken Leg! You are only one, and we are many. Come down!"

Eagle hooted in derision.

"How many dung eaters does it take to pull down an eagle?"

He strutted and posed along a level portion of the ledge, irritating the enemy as much as possible to make them careless.

At the same time his mind was racing. "You are only one—" Bull's Tail had signed. True, the Old Man was in the cave, still sleeping, Eagle supposed. The old recluse could sleep at any time. But was it possible the Head Splitters were completely unaware of the presence of a second man? It was puzzling. He tried to recall whether they had actually seen the Old Man at any time, but could not remember. The oldster could come and go so swiftly and quietly that even Eagle was amazed and confused. Again, he wondered if there was a secret cleft or passage which enabled the Old Man to come and go from the rock unseen. Maybe he was no longer in the cave at all.

Of course, there was one other thought. When the final push came, as it eventually must, of what use would the Old Man be? There was room on the ledge for only one man at a time. The second would be almost useless. Eagle realized that he had entirely abandoned the thought of any help from the Old Man. He had done so a number of times before, he recalled, and the Old Man had somehow turned up as he was needed. Ah, well, it was all water down the stream now.

A movement along the path caught his eye, and he saw the crouching shape of a warrior slip around the bulging rock and move cautiously upward. Eagle had seated himself in an inconspicuous place to wait. Now there were shouts from below, and the warriors on the other shore gestured, pointing out the position of the seated Eagle. The other warrior saw him now, rose to his full height, and stepped forward. Eagle, still seated, reached to the ground beside him to pick up the thong which lay there.

He had worked much of the night, cutting thin strips from the rawhide packs, joining them together, until he had a thong nearly thirty paces in length. Now, it lay extended along the path. He must wait until just the proper moment, then a quick jerk. If his trap worked properly, a sliding mass of stone, balanced precariously in a crevice along the trail, would crush the assailant or carry him over the edge.

Eagle's knuckles tightened on the thong. The approaching warrior had nearly stopped. He was suspicious, cautious, and seemed to sense something wrong. Eagle rose to his feet, and this seemed to reassure the other man. Now he came forward again.

Either Eagle's pull was a trifle early, or the other man saw the trap and leaped back. Perhaps both. The propping stick jerked free and loose stone came pouring and bouncing from the crevice. The boulders and broken rock, carried so secretly and carefully through the night, rattled to the path, some bounding high into the air above the river before plummeting downward.

Through the dust and debris, Eagle saw the other man laughing. The trap had failed. Now, in moments, the man would be able to scramble over the fallen stones. Eagle hurried to meet him.

And behind this warrior came another. A third could be seen rounding the bulge of the bluff.

Carefully, Eagle stepped toward his first opponent. There

was room for no mistakes now. One of the massive stone clubs so favored by the Head Splitters dangled from the warrior's right hand. Good. The man was right handed, and the sheer face of the bluff on his right would prevent a full swing. Eagle picked up a fist-sized rock as a secondary weapon and advanced.

He saw the man's eyes lift, focus above and beyond. It was an old trick, to make the opponent turn his head. Eagle refused to be deceived. Then there was a slight noise behind him, and at the same time the other warrior's mouth flew open in startled amazement.

Eagle stepped back, out of reach, and turned. There, descending the dead tree, were the two enemy warriors from the top of the bluff. It had been a diversion, a complicated plan to entrap him between the two groups of attackers. But something had gone wrong. The tree was moving, pivoting slowly on the ledge. Through the dust and debris, falling down the side of the bluff and past the cave's mouth, Eagle caught a glimpse of the Old Man. His back was braced against the rock, and one foot pushed powerfully on a branch which seemed to hold the giant tree in balance.

Slowly, the great trunk twisted and rolled, until it came free and slid across the ledge, with a thunderous roar and a cloud of dust. One of the men clinging tightly to the branches screamed as he fell, the other remained silent.

The dust began to settle before the cave, and Eagle thought the Old Man waved as he stepped back inside. He was never certain, because now he must turn his attention again to fighting for his life.

Even as he turned back to face the advancing warriors on the ledge, there was a heaviness in his heart that he had not expected. The falling of the great tree had removed all possibility of escape over the upper rim of the bluff. He was now committed to fight to the end here, where he now stood.

CHAPTER 32

Sweet Grass prepared food and fed her children, then left them at the lodge of their grandmother, the Tall One. She walked through the camp of the Elk-dog band, resolute in her errand. The young woman stopped before the lodge of the medicine man. She rapped on the skin lodge cover and called out.

"*Ah-koh!* Willow, are you there?"

Her sister-in-law swung back the door flap, smiling, and motioned her inside. They exchanged greetings, and the visitor sat. There was a moment of uncomfortable silence, and then Willow spoke.

"You are troubled, my sister?"

Sweet Grass nodded.

"I would talk with you and Owl."

"He will be back soon."

The two talked of small things and watched the two children of Willow and Owl play near the fire. Owl returned from tending his horses and entered the lodge.

"*Ah-koh*, sister, welcome to our lodge!"

The medicine man did not fail to note the serious expressions on the faces of the women. He sat, leaned against the willow backrest, and lighted his pipe with a twig from the lodge fire.

"It is well with you, sister?"

He could tell that all was not well, but wished to give her the chance to talk. He knew that she faced a major decision.

Sweet Grass heaved a long sigh.

"Not really, my brother."

She hesitated, unsure how to begin.

"It is six moons my husband has been missing."

Owl nodded.

"Yes, my sister. You know that you are welcome in our lodge."

He and Willow had discussed this matter long and seriously. It was not uncommon among the People to take more than one wife. Usually, it was for a reason such as this. Men were killed in the hunt or in battle. Someone must care for the wives and families, to provide food and shelter, and it was logical for close relatives to do so. So, some lodges, usually those of the most affluent warriors, might have two or even three wives.

Willow and Sweet Grass were close friends. More like sisters, actually. They shared a reflected recognition as wives of the chief's two sons. Yet Willow was not certain she could deal with this new problem. How would she react, she asked herself honestly, to the thought of her friend sharing her husband's bed?

It was not a pleasant prospect. Willow and Owl had had a very special relationship, ever since they met as prisoners of the Head Splitters. To share him with another?

Next moment Willow would feel ashamed, selfish, that she would deny her friend the shelter of their lodge. Of course, she could live with such an arrangement. Many women had done so. She, Willow, would, of course, be the primary wife, the sit-by companion to her husband. She would be his assistant in the carrying out of his medicine man duties.

Willow had frankly told her husband of her doubts. They had no secrets from each other. But in the end her sense of right led her to leave open the invitation.

Her private wishes, unspoken even to Owl, were that Sweet Grass would find another lodge. She could return to her own parents' lodge in the Mountain band. Or she could easily accept the attention of any one of the young men of the Elk-dog band. There would be several possibilities. Four Bears, though not exciting, would be a good provider.

But Sweet Grass was speaking.

"No, Owl, it is not that. You know I am not ready. I have never felt that Eagle is dead."

Owl nodded again. He knew that the girl was reluctant to accept the loss of her husband. She still thought of him as missing, not dead.

Owl had tried to help her approach the matter realistically. There was little possibility, even if his brother had survived the stampede, that he could have wintered alone and remain alive. The People had searched long and far and found no trace. The entire landscape had been trampled to tatters by sharp hooves. After three suns, the search had been abandoned. There was little hope of finding the missing warrior, either dead or alive. If he were alive, he would find his way back to the People. If not, well, he should fare well in the Spirit-World. He had been a bold and proud warrior, a credit to his tribe.

But Sweet Grass had completely refused to accept that possibility. She resisted all suggestions that her husband could not, in all reasonable probability, be alive.

Owl was hard put to pursue the argument, because in truth he felt the same. He had never confided this, because his head told him his brother could not have survived. Still, his heart told him that Eagle lived.

Sweet Grass was continuing.

"It is not that, my brother. It is the dreams I have had."

"Tell me, Sweet Grass."

She dropped her eyes, puzzled and confused.

"I dream of eagles. Birds, not Eagle, my husband."

Owl was startled by her revelation, because he had been troubled by such dreams himself. He had not been able to interpret their meaning.

"What is your vision, sister?"

"I always see an eagle circling and looking across the prairie. Then there is another eagle, but this one never flies."

She stopped, still confused.

"I do not know. I think this other eagle cannot fly. It is on a big rocky place."

"Why does it not fly, sister?"

Sweet Grass shrugged helplessly.

"It might be trapped or injured. Do you know, Owl?"

He shook his head. Some things were beyond his understanding as a medicine man.

"Do you think this might be a dream of my husband?"

"I do not know, sister. But there is some meaning if we can find it. I too have been dreaming of eagles."

Quietly, he told of his own vision, of a young eagle learning to fly, while an older bird circled anxiously overhead. They could still find no meaning.

"Tell me more, Sweet Grass, of the place you see, where the eagle is."

"It is not clear, brother. I only see it as a high, rocky place. Gray, I think. The eagle moves but cannot leave."

"*Why* does it not leave? Is it injured?"

The confused look crossed her face again.

"I cannot tell. It moves well. Could it be tied?"

Medicine men of the People sometimes kept a tethered eagle or hawk as part of their equipment.

"I do not know, sister. The other bird, the one who flies, is it a medicine animal? Does it hold the eagle prisoner?"

"No, I think not, Owl. I think it wants to help the other one. What is your dream?"

Owl shook his head.

"No, yours is much clearer. I only see an eagle struggling to fly. Yours must be a strong vision. There is meaning here."

He was puzzled. An eagle, captive in some way, trying to leave or fly from a high, rocky place. What could it mean? And what of the other eagle?

Sweet Grass was struggling with the half-formed thoughts from her dream.

"I think," she hesitated, "I think the eagle is in danger."

Owl had begun to have the same uncomfortable feeling.

"My husband," Willow interjected, "we have said that your brother, Eagle, will return if he is alive. Could this be a sign that he wishes to, but cannot? That he is in danger?"

Both the others had reached the same conclusion at nearly the same time.

"Yes," nodded Owl. "This must be it. Sweet Grass, you have had the strongest visions because your spirit is closer to his than any other. Can you remember any more about the place in your dream?"

Frantically, the girl shook her head.

"No, no, I have told you all. High rocks, gray rocks."

"And grass. You said the other eagle flies over prairie."

"Yes. Grass and trees. There are trees."

"Water? Where there are trees there must be water."

"Yes!" Sweet Grass was excited now. "There is water below!"

"Do you know the place, Owl?" Willow spoke excitedly.

"No, but there are cliffs along the Head-Split River."

He was trying to remember the days of his study under the old medicine man, White Buffalo. Something about that area. The People seldom camped there. There had been, before Owl was born, a massacre of four young men of the People by a band of Head Splitters. The event had changed the name of the stream, formerly Sycamore River.

But that was not the reason it was avoided. What was it that old White Buffalo had told him? That it was a place of the spirits?

"Bad medicine, Uncle?" young Owl had asked.

The old medicine man grunted.

"Not good or bad. Just strong."

This must be the explanation. Owl became almost enthusiastic at the prospect.

"Eagle must be in need. We will go to find him!"

It was not unheard of for a medicine man of the People to organize a hunting or war party, but it was somewhat unusual. It was more unusual for a woman to ride with the party, as Sweet Grass insisted she would do.

The two went to find Standing Bird, leader of the Elk-dog Society. They would need warriors. The exact nature of the trouble they faced was in doubt.

Standing Bird offered the services of his entire Warrior Society, and word spread rapidly. The party must move quickly, according to the medicine man, though even he was not completely certain why. The two other Warrior Societies would remain in defense of the village.

By the time Sun Boy was exactly overhead, the search party was ready to move.

CHAPTER 33

They rode four abreast, the leaders of the party. Sweet Grass and Owl were in the middle, flanked by Standing Bird and Heads Off. The chief had insisted on accompanying the search party for his son.

Owl, as medicine man, had determined the direction of travel. They would start from the scene of the hunt the previous fall, and follow the general direction of the stampede. They had made this search before, but now they would swing farther to the south and locate Head-Split River. There they would cross and follow the stream. The bluffs, Owl believed, were on the north bank, and they could better see and examine the rocky heights from across the river.

Throughout all of this, he had made clear to the girl at his side that if she saw, heard, or even felt in her mind anything that might be of importance, she was to speak.

Owl had attempted to guess how far this journey might take them. He had no idea how long his brother had clung to the wildly running horse, unable to escape the press of the stampede. How far could a strong young elk-dog run before collapsing? And what then?

"You know, Sweet Grass, that we may find only his bones. Maybe the eagle is captive because it is only a spirit, with no means to fly."

The girl nodded.

"I know, my brother, but I do not think so in my heart."

Moving as rapidly as was reasonable and still spare the horses, they crossed a vast expanse of prairie before Sun Boy finished his daily run. It was decided to camp for the night and push ahead by first light.

They stiffly dismounted and started campfires. Anxious, impatient, and irritable over the time being wasted in the search, Sweet Grass walked ahead on foot, to the top of the next rise. Perhaps she could see the river from there.

She heard a step behind her and turned quickly. It was her father-in-law, Heads Off.

"You must not wander off alone, little one," he chided her. "It would not be good to find the son but lose his wife."

"I know, Uncle," she apologized, using the term of respect for any adult male of the People. "I am only so impatient to find him."

"Yes, I, too," he nodded. His eyes misted a little. "Only now do I understand my father's feelings when I was thought dead."

"Do you think Eagle is dead?"

"I do not know, daughter. But," he paused to point at the campfires blossoming in the meadow below, "many of us have enough doubts to be here."

He smiled at her. Both his sons had married well. Heads Off never ceased to admire the spirit and determination of the women of his adopted people. Here was this slim girl, ready to ride into the unknown, ready to fight for her husband's life.

She was standing, gazing at the sunset. Sun Boy was spilling his finest colors across earth's rim. Sweet Grass tilted her head back to see the orange-pink sky overhead and suddenly stiffened.

High above circled an eagle, curving lower and lower with each spiral. Fascinated, she watched.

"My chief," she whispered, "it is the bird of my vision!"

The soaring creature dropped to a level not far above the hill and on fixed wings shot past their heads, a piercing scream cutting the quiet twilight. From that point, its course never wavered. Straight as an arrow the eagle flew, on and on, out of sight in the distance.

"That is the bird," she repeated. "I know it. It can be no other."

She turned and was running, back toward the camp.

"Owl!" she screamed. "I have seen it! The eagle!"

Here and there, warriors exchanged embarrassed glances. *Aiee*, there was nothing unusual in seeing an eagle! Perhaps the wife of the missing man had gone mad.

But Owl, the medicine man, was very serious.

"Tell me, sister, how it came. You had a vision?"

"No, no, a real flying bird. Your father saw it, too!"

"But how do you know it was the bird of your vision? One eagle looks much like another."

"This was different, Owl, I *know* this is the one. It flew down low over us and spoke to me."

Owl was ready to admit that this could happen.

"What did the eagle say?"

"No words, my brother. It only cried out."

Heads Off nodded.

"It is as she says."

"Come. Show me!"

The three walked quickly to the hilltop and stood in the fading light.

"It came from above and flew away, straight as an arrow, that way. We must follow."

Sweet Grass was insistent. She could see no reason to delay.

"But, little sister," Owl protested, "it is growing dark."

"And my husband needs us!"

The girl was practically in tears. In the end, it was her determination that caused the Elk-dog warriors to extinguish their fires and move on. These were men of her own age, friends of her husband. They had all played together as children. Only two or three were older, the very first warriors of the People to learn the ways of elk-dog medicine.

Now the belief of Sweet Grass was so strong that it affected the others. As they moved on, there was not a man who doubted that their fellow warrior, Eagle, was alive and that they must push ahead to help him.

The night was not yet fading to gray dawn when they came to a good-sized stream.

"Sweet Grass, we must stop," Owl pleaded. "We cannot see to cross."

Reluctantly, they camped. Few slept. They watched the Seven Hunters wheel slowly across the dark sky, until finally there was a smudge of pale gray in the east.

The party began to stir, and warriors moved up and down the stream, seeking the best crossing. They selected a shallow riffle and by first light splashed across to follow the course of the wandering stream.

The prairie was coming alive in the Moon of Awakening. Touches of green showed on distant hills. On a rise to their left, prairie grouse drummed their courtship dance, and on a hillside where the dead grass had grown sparsely, white dog-tooth flowers shone in profusion.

Heads Off remembered, with a warm comfortable feeling, that he had brought a tiny bouquet of the dog-tooth to his wife, the Tall One, during their courtship. This flower had been a special thing for them ever since.

Owl meanwhile was busily observing the state of the prairie. It would soon be time for the medicine man to announce the time for the burning of the grass. Such things must go on, regardless of the outcome of this search. The burning at the proper time was essential to the return of the grass and the buffalo, the basis of the People's existence.

But for Sweet Grass, nothing was important except the search ahead. She rode in front of the others, straining her eyes ahead to see any trace of rocky cliffs.

As it occurred, she was not the one to see the river bluff

first. She had raised her eyes to watch a speck in the sky
ahead, which circled and grew larger, finally becoming recog-
nizable as an eagle.

"Look!" Sweet Grass exclaimed.

At almost the same instant, Standing Bird pointed.

"Look!"

The object of his interest appeared as a darker shade of blue
in the blue haze of the distant ranges of rolling hills.

"The bluffs!"

They quickened their pace, pushing rapidly forward. The
reason for the urgency was not clear to any of the warriors. It
only seemed appropriate.

To Sweet Grass, however, it became more and more apparent as she rode. Though her husband had been missing for
many moons, now was the time of decision. He was in danger,
and only their timely arrival could save him.

From time to time she caught sight of the eagle as it circled
and screamed its high whistling cry. Some would have said
that the bird was only voicing protest against the unfamiliar
sight of a war party invading its nesting territory. Some in the
party might have thought so. But for Sweet Grass this was the
bird of her vision, leading the way to her husband's place of
imprisonment.

Imprisonment? She was not certain. At this point the sym-
bolism of dream became obscure. It was with a bit of dread
that she pushed forward, uncertain of what they would find on
the gray bluffs that loomed ahead. She only knew that they
must hurry.

They lost sight of the bluffs for the time as they skirted
around a heavy growth of timber along the river. Three deer
jumped from the fringe of brush before them to bound over
the hill.

Suddenly, Standing Bird, riding beside the girl, signaled for
a halt and held up a hand for silence. From the woods came

the muffled whinny of a horse. They turned cautiously aside and found a band of horses tied among the trees. The animals were saddled, and the equipment indicated only one thing.

"Head Splitters!"

Standing Bird signed rather than speaking and then silently signaled to advance.

The party soon heard shouts ahead and pushed their way out of the timber into an area of open meadow, to see warriors along the stream.

Standing Bird's horsemen spurred forward, completely surrounding four Head Splitters before they realized what had happened. It was only then, with the greater visibility, that the entire confused scene began to unfold for the newcomers.

The river at this point appeared wide and deep. The men along this shore had been watching something along the side of the stark gray bluff opposite. There were men on a narrow ledge there, high on the rock, above the tops of the great trees that grew from the river's edge.

But, at that moment, the attention of all was distracted by a grinding, splitting sound from higher along the cliff. The eyes of everyone, even those on the ledge, turned to watch a great dead tree pivot slowly and slide over the rim to plunge downward. Two helpless men clung pitifully to the branches of the falling giant. One screamed as it fell.

The river's calm was shattered as the great tree crashed to the earth, partly in the water. The tiny clinging figures were thrown like toys into the willows at the bluff's base. The dust began to settle, and there was a quiet trickle and splash of loose stones, dislodged by the giant's fall.

But now attention was drawn back to the ledge. It appeared that three men from below were climbing to attack a fourth. The lone man, braced to meet the attackers, appeared familiar.

"Eagle!" the girl spoke softly. It was essential not to distract the combatant at this critical moment. One glance aside could be fatal.

Standing Bird was signing to his warriors, bringing up those with bows to assist the beleaguered Eagle. The first bowman had not yet loosed his arrow, however, when the men on the ledge grappled in combat.

The Head Splitter, hampered in his club's swing by the closeness of the bluff's face, attempted to swing a backhand blow. Eagle dodged, and the club smashed against the rock. The Head Splitter recovered quickly and struck again, but Eagle again stepped back and counterthrust with his knife. The other man parried the blow and grasped the wrist, swinging his club again. Desperately, Eagle grasped the arm that held the club, and the two wrestled along the ledge.

The bowmen below could not shoot for fear of striking Eagle. They could only watch helplessly as the two locked in mortal combat.

Then the inevitable happened. One or the other, seeking solid footing on the narrow ledge, did not find it. The weight of the struggling pair overbalanced. It happened quickly. One moment the two wrestled on the bluff, the next they were plunging downward, still locked together in a deathlike grip.

Only now did Sweet Grass scream her husband's name.

CHAPTER 34

"Eagle!"

As he plunged downward, Eagle could have sworn he heard the voice of his wife call his name. In the confusion of his thoughts, it seemed only one more of the unexplained mysteries that he had encountered since his plunge from the cliff many moons ago.

Again, he had a momentary thought that since that fall, he had been already dead. He had wandered in a strange Spirit-World peopled by bears that walked like a man and a real-cat that brought him food. There were also enemies and dreams and memories, which included the sounds of his wife's voice.

Now he was falling again. Or was he still falling? Had all the moons of the winter been only a vision, passing in an instant between wakefulness and the sleep-world? Had the Old Man been only a ridiculous dream?

The struggling pair, falling from a slightly different portion of the ledge, were not directly over the big sycamore. Its outer branches whipped the falling bodies, and Eagle's eyes involuntarily closed tightly to prevent injury. He felt as though someone were striking him repeatedly across the face, chest, and arms with a quirt, bringing blood with each blow.

His eyes were still closed when the two struck the water, with a slap like the tail of a gigantic beaver. He plummeted to the depths, no longer feeling the body of the other man. The river's bottom rushed up at him, rocks smashing at his arm and shoulder. Then he was fighting for life, trying to rise, choking, dying for air, swimming, clawing upward toward the sunlight, which seemed now so far above.

He must have lost consciousness, for he was only dimly aware of hands taking hold of his arms, shoulders, and head, dragging him from the water. Drifting in and out of reality, Eagle marveled again at the strange spirit-medicine of the gray bluff. Only a moment ago, he had been alone, surrounded by enemies and fighting for his life. Now, a few heartbeats later, he was among his friends and family.

They carried him to a soft robe, covered him with another, while Sweet Grass held and rocked him gently in her arms. Her tears splashed on his face, warm and salty after the coldness of the dark river.

Aiee, Eagle thought, now he really must be dead. How else could he be transported to his own?

The thing which made him doubt, however, was that he continued to choke, coughing and vomiting large quantities of water. At times it seemed that he would never be able to take the next breath. He drifted to sleep again, the paroxysm of choking temporarily quiet.

Meanwhile, the Elk-dog warriors were busy, up and down the stream. Two of the bowmen with Bull's Tail tried to fight and were quickly cut down. The third threw down his weapons.

Standing Bird shouted and signed to the two on the ledge to come down, and seeing no alternative, they moved to do so.

Bull's Tail leaned against a tree, completely dejected. He had made not one move to pick up a weapon. How could things be worse? There were only four men left alive of his entire party, and these were prisoners. Everything he had attempted had failed. His medicine must indeed have been bad to begin with on this war party. Either that, or somehow the spirit-medicine of this cursed gray stone was against him.

Owl strode up to speak to the dejected chief.

"So, Bull's Tail, we meet again!"

He had learned the Head Splitters' tongue while he was their prisoner some years before.

Bull's Tail looked at the young medicine man, puzzled.

"Do I know you? How is it that you speak my tongue?"

"I learned it as your prisoner. You do not remember?"

"*Aiee*, you are that one? Then this one is your brother?"

He indicated the semiconscious Eagle.

Owl nodded.

"It is no wonder, then, that he has been a thorn in my flesh. Had I realized, I might have understood our troubles and avoided him entirely. You two are bad medicine."

Owl's father walked over to confront the captive chief.

"And," continued Bull's Tail, "this is your father. Your family has turned my world to dung, Hair Face!"

Heads Off, known as "Hair Face" to the enemy, understood none of their language, but the two had met before. He nodded in recognition.

"Owl, ask him where they found your brother."

Owl relayed the question.

"Right at this spot, four suns ago," answered the dejected chief. "Our medicine has been bad ever since. You may as well kill us now. There is nothing left for us."

Owl chuckled and shook his head, then translated for his father and Standing Bird, who had approached.

"My father, this man treated me fairly when I was his prisoner and kept others from killing me. We should let him go."

"As you wish, my son. The others, too?"

"Why not?" Standing Bird interjected. "They can carry the word that the People can be reasonable as well as strong." Heads Off nodded.

"It is good."

Bull's Tail would have argued. It would be preferable, he felt, to be killed by a superior force, than to return to his tribe in disgrace, having lost his war party, not in combat, but to a series of seemingly unconnected misfortunes and errors of judgment.

The thing that eventually stopped his argument, however, was a glance at the brooding gray bluff. What would happen, he wondered, to the spirit of a man dying here? He had an uncomfortable feeling that perhaps a spirit released here would be trapped here for all eternity by the medicine of the rock. Surely, there could be a better time and place to die.

Shadows were lengthening now.

"Camp here tonight," Standing Bird suggested with sign talk. "Then we will all leave in the morning."

Reluctantly, Bull's Tail agreed. The surviving Head Splitters made their camp a little apart, and campfires were started.

A warrior trotted up to where Owl and his father were talking.

"Eagle is awake!"

They hurried over. Eagle lay with his head in the lap of his wife, smiling weakly. Only now was he able to talk, to ask questions, to relate to reality.

"How did you find me?"

Sweet Grass smiled.

"An eagle told me."

Eagle was too tired to inquire further. He would hear the entire story later.

Standing Bird was burning with curiosity.

"My brother, what happened to you? We saw you carried away on your horse in the stampede!"

"We fell over the bluff with many buffalo. My leg was broken."

There was a murmur of disbelief from the listeners. They looked up at the high rock and imagined what such a fall could do.

"And you have been here ever since?" Owl demanded. "How did you find food? Where did you spend the winter?"

Eagle took a deep breath. There was much to tell, and just now he felt very weak and tired.

"The Old Man helped me."

"The old man? What old man?"

Owl was puzzled, and Eagle was frustrated.

"You have not talked to the Old Man?"

"We have seen no one, Eagle, except the Head Splitters."

Weakly, Eagle raised his head.

"I wintered in his cave. There!" He pointed to the rocky cliff. "The Old Man helped me escape. He pushed the tree over the ledge."

A sudden thought struck him. Had the Old Man been injured in the fall of the tree? Was he lying now, hurt or dying, in the cave?

"Send someone to see," he urged. "He is in the cave at the top of the ledge."

The light was fading, but there was yet time. Two young warriors swam across and started up the path. Owl, suspicious that his brother might be delirious, went to talk to Bull's Tail.

"Was my brother alone when you found him?"

The chief nodded.

"Yes. We found no one else. I know someone must have helped him through the winter, but we could not find them."

"You did not see anyone else on the ledge? No one pushed the tree?"

"Of course not! The tree fell when they tried to climb down and shook it loose!"

"But you think there was someone else with him?"

"I did think so, but I was mistaken. We saw no one. Whoever helped him through the winter must have gone." Bull's Tail shrugged. "Why should I care?"

Owl had sought answers and had now only more questions. Had there been another man, or had there not? If so, who could the man have been? And, why, Owl wondered, was his brother so vague about it? He returned to where Eagle lay.

"My brother, tell me more of this old man. Is he of the People?"

"No, he has no tribe."

"Everyone has a tribe, Eagle."

Eagle was sore, irritable, and becoming tired of pointless questions.

"He said he has no tribe, Owl. Ask him yourself!"

He was becoming more concerned now. If the Old Man was unhurt, why had he not shown himself at the cave entrance? Did he simply wish to avoid people? Much as Eagle had disliked, almost hated, the old recluse at times, he hoped nothing had happened to him. And now he was sorry for having spoken so harshly to his brother.

"Owl," he offered, "you will have to see for yourself about the Old Man. He is very different. He may be an outcast, but I do not know his tribe."

He omitted his suspicions from time to time that the oldster might be the legendary Old Man of the Shadows. Here, in the light of day, in the presence of other people, such thoughts seemed ridiculous. It was surely just from being alone that his mind had played tricks on him. Never mind. It would be interesting to see Owl's reaction to the old recluse when he came down.

The warriors were climbing past the narrow part of the ledge now, working their way upward. All those below watched anxiously. Curiosity as to Eagle's companion was growing as the two neared the point where Eagle had indicated the cave.

Sweet Grass leaned back and happily studied the sky just above the rocky rim. She admired the colors Sun Boy was using tonight to celebrate the return of her husband. In the far pink of the sky, an eagle circled, and Sweet Grass smiled.

Now the warriors disappeared behind the scrubby fringe of dogwood. The watchers on the ground waited, anxious for them to reappear. Eagle became impatient, finally pushing forward to sit up.

"*Ah-koh!*" he shouted. "Is he all right?"

There was no immediate answer, but in a few moments, one of the men appeared on the ledge. He stood, looking down at those waiting below. He appeared perplexed.

"Eagle," he shouted, "is there another cave? There is no one here. This cave is empty!"

CHAPTER 35

Among the People, it was said afterward that Eagle had changed from his ordeal on the gray bluff, now called Medicine Rock by his tribe. No trace had been found of the old man Eagle spoke of so insistently. Some thought he had been only a product of the imagination, brought on by pain and suffering.

Eagle was still an able warrior, though he always limped a little from the old injury. His hair, black as a crow's wing, began to gray. He and his brother, the medicine man, seemed to have a closer relationship than before. In fact, Eagle appeared to have developed a closeness, an understanding relationship with everyone. It was as if he had developed an insight into the problems of others.

He and Sweet Grass spent a long and comfortable life together, one of the happiest appearing couples in the Elk-dog band. Their children grew strong and straight.

It was always said of Eagle that there was no one with a stronger link to his medicine animal, his spirit-guide. His was a sensitivity, an understanding that exceeded all, with the possible exception of the medicine man himself.

Most of all, though, in the newly found spirit of Eagle, was his way with children. He had always been active in teaching the youngsters of the Rabbit Society but now became even more so. Not only his own children, but any child of any age seemed drawn to him. He became their favorite storyteller.

When darkness would fall, across the prairie, and the story fires were lighted, the children would gather round, casting fearful yet expectant glances at the black wall of the night. Someone would go to ask Eagle to come, and he would keep the listeners entranced far into the night with many tales of long ago. Tales of when the world was young and the bobcat had a long tail.

Even then, the Trickster, the Old Man of the Shadows, had been old, Eagle said. And his descriptions of the Trickster were so vivid, so real, that the listener almost felt that Eagle had been there himself.

Don Coldsmith is a physician who lives near Emporia, Kansas. In addition to his Spanish Bit novels, he writes a syndicated column on horses and country living, and is a breeder of Appaloosa horses. He is the 1983 president of the Western Writers of America. His *Elk-dog Heritage* was one of three finalists for the Golden Spur award as Best Western Novel of 1982.

So far, five novels in the Spanish Bit Saga have been published as Double D Westerns: *Trail of the Spanish Bit, Buffalo Medicine, The Elk-dog Heritage, Follow the Wind,* and *Man of the Shadows.*